The Executioner's Art reflects David Fine's first trade as an archaeologist: stripping things down to reveal their origins. Born in Coventry and brought up in Cheltenham, David now lives in Bakewell with his wife and daughter. He co-ordinates Lit-Net, works as a poet and as an arts facilitator. His author credits range from *A Complete Guide to the French Revolution 1789–1989* to *A History & Guide to Sheffield*, but *The Executioner's Art* marks his debut as a novelist.

First published in 2002 by
Tindal Street Press Ltd
217 The Custard Factory, Gibb Street, Birmingham B9 4AA
www.tindalstreet.org.uk

The cover design of *The Executioner's Art* was inspired by the work
of sculptor Johnny White, particularly 'Barking up the Wrong Tree'
at the Millennium Gallery, Sheffield.

Copy Editor: Penny Rendall
Typesetting: Tindal Street Press Ltd

A CIP catalogue reference for this book is available from
the British Library.

ISBN: 0 9541303 1 6

Printed and bound in Great Britain by
Biddles Ltd, Woodbridge Park Estate, Guildford.

The Executioner's Art

David Fine

TINDAL STREET PRESS

To Kay and Laurel

Acknowledgements

Countless people have helped see this book through from an idea in my head to the words you read now. Perhaps not quite such a long list as the credits to a film, and we're loath to include postal services that don't deliver. However, there are agents, readers, editors, designers – it's not just a writer alone. Here I'd like to thank in particular Richard, Neil, Jackie, Emma, Alan and Penny with all my heart.

Part One

'Do not fall asleep in your enemy's dream.'

Xhosa saying
(quoted in *The Cattle Killing* by John Edgar Wideman)

One

This is a city where rivers disappear. The rain almost reluctantly blurred into snow, slowing down, holding up, filling the darkness between the street lights' wet yellow glow with silence. Each glow grew smaller, further away, colder: a strange reptile's eye determining which colour and shape the rest of its strange scaly skin should take. At certain moments Sheffield becomes a creature its inhabitants rush to hide from. People only see it inside their heads when they come close to evil.

Tyres slushed and slithered over the creature's slimy back. Two beat officers in a local patrol car took a shortcut down towards their station. They were late and tired: their night duties had been hard. The patrol car stopped. Within the fallen snow its headlights had crossed a set of tyre tracks running into the yard of a small empty factory.

On dark hills far away the weather beacons had forecast snow, but not its intensity. The beacons could not stop the snow, nor understand its intentions as the officers stepped from their car.

The moon disappeared from view as they shivered inside their sleek luminescent traffic coats, their dark uniforms buttoned up against the cold of the night. The snow flecked their boots. They said nothing, just shuffled closer together, trying to hide from a simple fear of the undiscovered.

In a strange reptile's eyes we must seem peculiar too – perhaps full of hidden threats. The police officers' flashlights, two large eyes, followed the set of tyre tracks that slithered away from the empty yard. At the far end of these tyre tracks an engine stalled. Its driver had to stop and listen. He heard a creature breathe hard inside his head. He watched the windscreen wipers whirr more slowly under load. The driver squirmed round to face the slanted corrugated roofs of dead foundries and metal shops. The buildings leant into each other down a treeless valley.

Inside the yard broken tears froze within the driver's tyre tracks, became hard, dirty ice, to block corroded gutters yet staunch old seeping wounds. The two beat officers stepped through the thickening snow to enter the empty factory. They slid into each other and half fell over, almost like the buildings around them.

Fluid and earth leaked into each other beneath the officers' beat and the creature's dark belly. Drains gurgled and croaked, slobbered and drooled into five invisible rivers. Black, kinked, these twisted through the guts of the city. Into this wintry faecal dungeon flowed a little blood, viscera and bruised sand. A shred of identity scoured from an empty building. The slight smell of seared flesh lingered in the cold.

The officers held their breath at the open door, then entered.

Below the street lights' contused glow, other drivers slushed through the falling snow to avoid a stationary vehicle. Its driver did not try to restart his engine. He realized he had no need to hurry. He had left the empty building behind in a rush. No one seemed to notice, no one had followed. No one else would dare stop on a night like this: tap on a window to offer help. He tried to scream. He tried to cry. He had to escape the creature inside his brain that was devouring his thoughts.

The empty building hid the screams of the two beat officers. Held them in as they screamed at each other and the flash-lit carnage in the blackness below the corrugated roof.

The night moved on inside the dark. This is a city where people are cast down before they die.

Two

The light next morning fell from the tall windows of the church onto its congregation. Out of breath, Detective Constable Wilet tried to step quietly past the vestry to a space in the last row of pews. The singing of hymns had ushered her in; the snowy rows of gravestones outside seemed to mouth each chorus. Despite the weather, the church was packed. She had rushed through the snow and ice from where she had managed to park her car. Would she recognize the back of his head?

As she stretched her own neck to look, a sharp old woman tried to hand her a hymn book. She mouthed a No thank you, but the woman insisted. 'A hundred and sixty-two,' she mouthed back, 'third verse.' 194, 187, 155, 163: fingers still cold, DC Wilet flicked through the thin pages, half an eye still attempting to locate the back of his head. It was the same when she had phoned. 'You've just missed him. I am sorry,' his wife had replied. 'A mobile? It'll be set for message only; he wouldn't want it to ring inside the church.' Nothing for it but drive out here, and again she was too late. The service had begun.

The hymn ended just as Wilet found the right line. 'We never sing the final verse,' the old woman whispered. 'You're not looking for someone?'

'Detective Inspector Tilt,' DC Wilet whispered back. The old woman's face disapproved. It declared this was the wrong answer. It stated that the proper reason people came to church was to look for God, not policemen.

'John has failed to join us today,' the sharp woman explained, a hand shepherding her away from the congregation. 'He's had to take Sunday school at the vicarage. The large house to the right. You passed it on your way in.'

Its bell push didn't seem to work, but the unlocked door opened of its own accord. The smell of damp, disrepair, something not done mixed with the fresh wintry air. Children's voices, in ones or twos, clambered across the hallway, monkey arms grabbing onto banisters, to keep feet off the cold tiled floor. She had learnt this game as a kid too, and her winter shoes deftly chose a diagonal of white tiles running towards a door at the back of the hall. The children's voices stopped at her knock.

Detective Inspector Tilt sat in a dining chair by a french window, at ease with the children on the floor in front of his feet. Ruth Wilet remembered the DI from about five years ago. He appeared to have scarcely changed, just grown five years older. His straight brown hair had already started to thin long ago, but there wasn't a midriff bulge like most middle-aged detectives. It seemed odd yet right that he should take a Sunday school class. He didn't look like a policeman; his nose seemed too narrow, his jaw too delicate, a faraway slightly bemused stare to his pale eyes. 'I'll deal with this,' John Tilt said, to the children as much as to DC Wilet. He asked for two volunteers to fetch Miss Brookes from the church and sent ahead the two whose hands went up the slowest. He stepped along the sides of the room, very quietly, arms solemn, head down, checking for invisible obstacles in his path. He had remained a cautious man.

'Constable –?' he whispered in the doorway.

'Wilet, sir. On placement,' she whispered back. What was it about organized religion that made ordinary conversations occur in whispers? There was little call for organized religion at any of the police stations she knew – they had enough whisperers. 'Sorry to trouble you, sir. Chief Inspector Naylor phoned in with the flu and it's a serious incident.'

'There's a lot of it about.' Tilt did not make it clear whether he meant flu or serious incidents. 'You were fortunate to find my wife at home. Our youngest's full of cold, otherwise we'd all be here.'

Miss Brookes appeared, a child on each arm like stabilizer wheels on a kid's top-heavy bike. 'You've found John, I see.'

'Thank you, Miss Brookes,' Tilt replied for them both, as they each sidled through the door. The two children had already let go of her hands in order to join the others on the floor.

Ruth Wilet followed his steps back over the diagonal tiles into the snow and the streets. Inside the church they had stopped singing. She wondered why the children couldn't join the congregation. Perhaps it was the sort of church that frowned on babies crying at the baptismal font.

DI Tilt stared at a street full of parked cars. 'This isn't normal,' he said. 'Our vicar's about to retire. This is his final Sunday.'

It explained why the church had been so full.

Walking back to the car, DI Tilt listened carefully to the seriousness of the incident. They both seemed to make a point of stepping around small pairs of children's foot-prints left in the snow. 'It's cold,' he said, suddenly fastening up the collar of his ski coat. 'We'd better get back to Sodom and Gomorrah.'

Nothing more was said about the case. She asked if he wanted to pick up his own car. No, they didn't know when they'd finish, and he didn't want to leave his wife without transport. DC Wilet gave herself a ticking-off glance in the rear-view mirror; she knew few coppers who were that considerate on duty, if at all. They left the case alone. She worked out the best route to cross the city.

'You don't remember me, do you, sir?'

He hesitated. She had no lines edging her eyes then, her hair was less blond, less severe. 'Face but not the name, constable. You're right, I can't remember where. Sorry.'

She smiled. 'Probationary training. Five years ago. You delivered the CPS module "From Crime to Conviction".'

'Of course. How to get a result. Do you find practice matches theory?'

'No . . . yes . . . it's a little too early to say, sir.'

Tilt nodded his head. Despite all, he had begun to believe it was too late to tell. He wanted to say so, just as she wanted to ask why he had left the training school when he had so clearly enjoyed working there. Relative rank denied them the opportunity. The suddenness of his question had taken her unawares; it was easier to talk about the retirement of the local vicar. She was right, he did enjoy the training school. There was no need to say sorry: she was just one face among hundreds. Most became reliable police officers; she had been his professional future. A future which no longer seemed to exist.

'Just a moment, sir. I think that was our turning.'

DI Tilt wasn't sure. He thought Reddlewood's must have closed down years ago. In fact it had been placed under receivership the previous autumn, about the same time that City Police had shut their training school, forcing their detective inspector back to operations after seven years away.

DC Wilet parked their car next to the sector vehicle. They got out in an oily, debris-strewn yard. Rusting, half-finished foundry castings stood around, gradually turning into monstrous snowmen, not quite alive enough to die. Gravestones. Tilt would be forty-nine next birthday, a year away from full-pension retirement.

They did not discuss the case until they left the car. Tilt never did until the last possible moment. It was his personal insurance against a certain loss of feeling. He told a uniformed constable tightening the blue and white incident tape to fetch them all some tea and sandwiches. 'Buy extra,' he called across the yard. 'Enough for a dozen': forensics were hungry animals. Six loaves and twelve fishes might do it, with a bottle of Henderson's Relish thrown in. The thought of food left DI Tilt needing to hear that all was well at home.

They lived in a semi a peal of bells beyond the church. There was a noise on the line as his wife answered the phone. Tilt thought it was interference caused by the snow until she stopped the taps rushing against the stainless steel sink. Things were okay. Their youngest was still full of cold and had only just got out of bed. They needed to take the dog for a walk, which was her way of asking when he'd be back. John Tilt didn't know, but said nothing. Anything he said seemed to push them further apart. He dropped his phone into his ski-coat pocket.

Ruth Wilet thought the DI was a little embarrassed in her presence, having to call home like a dutiful child. Duty desk had radioed through the MO's update that the local beat officers were recovering in hospital from their initial shock, perhaps better than could be expected. No one could remember witnessing anything worse. They were cut off from the rest of the world. She followed him into the empty building.

'Is this your first murder investigation?' he asked at the half-open door. The padlock hasp had been forced: it and its padlock swung uselessly. The chromed thumbholes of the faded lever-arch files in the toolshop office had rusted away years ago, a process the smell of oil could not halt.

'No, sir,' she started to lie. She did not know why; it was her way of pretending it had never happened. She did not want anybody to die except when they needed to. And with the lie a dreadful terror rushed up her throat, a blind irrational belief that by investigating the death she had murdered the victim. She told Tilt the truth. 'No, sir. This is my first.'

He placed his hand very gently on her shoulder, like a priest or rabbi. 'It's a terrible feeling, I know, and it doesn't get better,' he whispered. 'It would be worse if it did.'

They stepped over the incident tape, through the office and up the cast-iron stairway onto the service gantry. Each step half-rang out like a broken bell. The snow drifted to fill the grooves of the corrugated roof, darkening the translucent panels above their heads. Below the gantry grating six blasting bays lay silent, three to each side of the passageway overhead. The trip switches to the three-phase motors which powered the machinery had been shut down. A safety helmet with a breathing mask and a crazed plastic visor lay empty on a fusebox. The compressors, sand and shot agitators, coolant emulsions and hydraulic taps stayed still. Their deafening noise of aggregate, air and liquid ganging up to thrash at rigid steel had vanished: poured down a sink, drained away into the past. The place had stopped. Become disconnected. It was as empty as an unvisited church. They moved as though they were inside one. The snow outside seemed to turn everything they dared touch inside out, stamping someone else's past into their future.

Beneath the roof neither of them pressed the gantry light switch: there was just enough daylight left to see. Tilt did not need to point; they knew where to look. A six-foot circular turntable, waiting to turn. Under the oversweet scent of spent hydraulic oil, fresh waves of abrasive particles lapped the turntable. Below their feet the local beat officers had earlier just managed to cloak the turntable itself with a regulation incident sheet, edged in blue and white. Shiny, all-purpose, inadequate. It trapped the slightly charred aroma of abraded flesh and the outline of a seated figure, waiting to turn. Beneath skin is blood.

Here and there floated discarded bloody scraps of worn-out visor, torn off when opaqued by abrasive. Tilt and Wilet examined them for prints. Their trained eyes simply recorded the residue of killing. But within their retinas each swirl of abrasive and sloughed scrap of visor grew into a picture of how the victim was probably murdered. Their bodies shivered till the gantry shook and the rest of the world stopped.

Ruth Wilet gripped the gantry rail – monkey arms grabbing banisters – as her eyes hurtled to the safety of a diagonal of lighter-coloured tiles. Tilt stared at the beat officers' bootprints which tied the incident sheet to the swirls of freshly spent abrasive. Snow thickened over the translucent panels.

Gently holding both her hands tight within his own, Tilt instructed Wilet to go back outside. To search very carefully for old tyre marks in the frozen snow before this latest fall obscured them.

'Find out how many vehicles were involved. Ask forensics, no, tell them to photograph and measure whatever you find. Go, now, quickly.' She repeated to herself each detail of her task. These instructions were her diagonal of lighter-coloured tiles.

He took the sector vehicle flashlight from his ski-coat pocket to sanction his way down into the sixth bay. He kept his feet close to the stair rail and along the wall, his head down: cautious, slow, tyres across ice, for fear his route would mask earlier tracks. Tilt's free hand raised a corner of the incident sheet.

'*Unto me is this grace given,*' he tried to quote to himself, '*that I should preach among the Gentiles the unsearchable riches of Christ; and to make all men see what is the fellowship of the mystery, which from the beginning of the world hath been hid in God, who created all things.*' He was too scared to swear at his Saviour. And too angry.

Minutes later a diesel engine clattered to a halt outside. The corner of the incident sheet fell and Tilt made his way back the way he had come. He took a last look through the gantry grating into blasting bay six. Each door of the van was slammed hard. Do investigating officers, he thought, ever shut them quietly?

From the toolshop office Tilt watched them record the tyre marks Wilet had observed, then surround the cardboard box lid of hot drinks and sandwiches which the uniformed constable had left on the bonnet of the sector vehicle. Falling snow settled onto their hats and shoulders, just like the half-finished castings outside in the yard, waiting to be sandblasted. John Tilt listened to them huddle around each other's twitches of conversation.

'Grisly,' said one.

'Gruesome,' another.

'Horrendous.'

Each breathed each word so slowly, restricting its sound and existence until the last possible moment, that each syllable split itself into a separate word, to dissect and thus sterilize its total meaning. It was almost calculated. They had heard all about the two local beat officers.

'Grotesque.'

'Too bloody grotesque.'

Tilt let them psych themselves up before calling across their liaison sergeant. After all, as their DI, he had only to watch them work inside. He explained that he required the entire site to be cordoned off, then the sixth bay dusted for foot and fingerprints.

'The whole floor,' the sergeant repeated. 'We'll be here all day.'

Tilt's eyes indicated the empty cardboard box lid on the sector vehicle's bonnet. 'Take your orders for lunch now, please,' he suggested. 'Nothing for me, thank you.'

The sergeant wasn't going to ask. He left to take the lid from the snow-decked bonnet, leaving its negative behind to be filled with more snow. Ruth Wilet watched them, her hands clenched around a beaker of cooling coffee above the tyre marks. Last night, when the suspects' vehicle had left its trail, her fingers had been free to sleep next to the warmth of her own body: whole, entire and safe, while the murderers' hands had left another body to grow cold and freeze.

In order to indicate the number of vehicles involved she raised a single finger to her detective inspector at the window of the toolshop office. He may not have noticed or understood. She and the liaison sergeant walked past each other, heads down in the falling snow and the cold. Their feet searched through the icy snow for the worn uneven cobbles below.

'You'd think that forensics would've learnt to bring packed lunches and thermos flasks by now,' Tilt remarked. He was right, but DC Wilet did not have the heart – or rank – to tell DI Tilt that they had been called scene of crime for at least three years. 'How many vehicles were you able to identify?'

'One,' she replied, lifting a finger once more away from the fragile plastic beaker. 'Either a car or a small van, sir.'

'Right. Good, well done.'

Rust from the gantry rail marked her single raised gloved finger. Snow had turned it into a stain. Her eyes climbed back up the cast-iron gantry stairs to the passageway. Step by step.

'Sorry, constable. You did say "one"?'

'Yes, sir. One.'

Tilt stared at the rusted thumbholes of the lever-arch files piled on top of a bent filing cabinet. His neck trembled slightly. Ruth Wilet realized that he had already looked underneath the regulation incident sheet.

'Would you prefer to help to locate the receivers?' he asked. 'At some point we will need to know how this place operated under normal conditions.'

She took a moment to shake her head. 'No, sir. That is, if it's all right by you, sir.'

'Of course, I'm sure it will be.'

Ruth Wilet wondered if the DI would have taken the same care of her if she were a man. Perhaps they were all too frightened to be left on their own. They watched scene of crime unfold their pristine white overalls in order to plot the aisles of a cross they would need to clear to the waiting turntable. SOCOs had already dusted the switches for prints but tired electric bulbs seemed to underline every shadow rather than light their scene. Bent over on hands and knees, dusting and lifting, bagging scraps of discarded visor and strange small squares of polythene, they discussed football, their cars, kids, what they did last night, other cases, anything to deny the sacrifice at the altar ahead. Come closer, said the cross, you need to know. The scene of crime officers fought the urge to break rank and flee, because they already knew.

'Is that coffee still warm, inspector? It doesn't matter if it isn't. I have a terrible head this morning. Terrible.'

Tilt handed over his cup with an unintended smile: it was a relief to hear a familiar voice. Hussein Yassire was the forensic pathologist. A devout Muslim, he and Tilt had found a bond in the strength of their personal faiths while discharging their duties in a less faithful world.

'You've stopped taking sugar, inspector.'

'Four years ago.'

'I have some in my bag. If you change your mind. Somewhere.'

Hussein Yassire talked as his hands delved. Quick, expert, clinical. His relationship with the police was odd; they only met as the direct result of death. A pathologist worked out the how so they could deal with the who – the deceased and the bereaved. He worked backwards, so they could move forwards. By determining the cause and time of death, his fingers came closest to turning back the hands of a broken clock, of bringing the dead back to life. The police had stolen him from medicine to do their dirty work, the nasty stuff, and in return he took the odd cup of cold coffee, which he turned sweet and sugary. With murders he transformed cold flesh into victims, not unlike wine into water.

Yassire was good at his job; Tilt knew, better than most policemen were at theirs. When they closed down the training school and sent him back to operations, John Tilt had been appalled but hardly surprised to overhear in the canteen and briefing rooms that the pathologist had gained the nickname of Fatwah. It was nearly a mark of respect.

'John, this coffee isn't cold, it's frozen. What do they do here? Blast away at metal with sand?'

'You'll see.'

The lifters of prints approached the end of their ordeal. Inch by inch they neared each corner of the incident sheet until they stretched up, polyester white knees stained slate grey, cold breath touching the centre of their white powder cross. Its dust contained marks from at least four pairs of shoes, after the elimination of Tilt's and the beat officers'. Tilt accepted the liaison sergeant's verbal report. There might be more, there could not be less. The body remained a single point of contact between two passing crowds of feet. The pool of abrasive seemed calm; amongst the debris blown about the room they had picked up the finest shreds

20

of skin: gossamer, icy, reptilian. Lifted from their victim and chucked away by spare compressed air. The direction of the cross would switch as soon as they lifted the incident sheet. Their investigation would also walk away from the body.

Police officers tend to remember faces and forget names as events brush past their careers. It is a visual endeavour: they slip photographs into their wallets, lockers and heads. They are trained and accustomed to classifying images. The DI gave the nod to raise the sheet: no time was right but their fingers and thumbs would only become colder, more liable to numb with shock. John Tilt felt his joints tighten. Ruth Wilet's hands rushed to touch her own cheeks and lips, to check they still existed.

Blue nylon rope still tied the remains to an office chair, its steel frame pitted yet shiny. Skin barely managed to survive even beneath the frayed strands of nylon – bruised, rubbed raw in the pain to escape. The victim had been sandblasted to death. Except perhaps under the chin or behind a knee, the murder had scoured away every layer of flesh.

Inside the empty building each harsh piece of embedded aggregate had pulped the corpse into the colour of night. From ears to toes, vestigial features and limbs were bonded in oil and blood, bits of rock and breath fused together. Silence. Last night the hum of three-phase motors had become a lethal trigger. Organs within the torso still oozed to escape: areas of the heart, liver and intestine were visible through broken membranes. Bones, pitted yet shiny, marked the site of hands, feet and ribs. Electric light picked out each eye-socket splattered with brain.

Red, yellow and grey.

The chair frame creaked as onlookers gagged back the urge to retch. An amalgam of blood, innards and tears had dripped out of the body, its flow chilled to dribbles of rime, glaciers of suffering.

Two men found it hard to breathe, a third rushed away

to vomit. They had unveiled a statue, a statue carved in flesh. Its stone eyes, lips and teeth ripped out, identity devoured. The face failed to exist, just a cold-blooded mutilation of the soul.

Everyone stood in shock. Hussein Yassire's hand crushed the cold plastic coffee beaker. The smoky smell of abraded flesh gagged those who looked away. Ruth Wilet's fingers rubbed a mole to the left of her nose. She was the only woman there. She wanted to chew her short straight hair, her fingernails, thumb. She stared at DI Tilt as though he were a mirror. He tried to close his eyes and remember his family. It didn't work; nothing worked.

Shock numbs pain; Ruth Wilet's teeth started to bite through her gloves. A little blood dropped from her mole rubbed raw. A murder planned, prepared and executed –

'Jesus Christ, they've crucified the fucking bastard.'

'Sergeant. This is a murder investigation.' Tilt hastily lockgated the whirling flood of anger inside his voice; they would all be sucked down if he did not keep control. 'This is a murder investigation. We each have a job to do,' he shouted. 'Okay? Any questions? Good. I'm sorry, please go back to work.'

They obeyed because they were trained to. No one dared offer to help replace the incident sheet. They did not return to talk of last night either, could not. Each wanted to run away with their screams trapped inside someone else's head. Instead fear twisted itself into hatred which vectored in on their detective inspector. Let him solve this bloody mess. It was his job.

Between shivers Hussein Yassire tried to view the skinless body with clinical detachment. He discovered his mind could not remember the call-out number for forensic pathology. 'Dead,' he whispered to the DI as much as to himself. 'Definitely dead. You're paying me to tell you this.'

'Thanks. I know,' replied Tilt as they finally turned away from replacing the incident sheet. He viewed a crack near the centre of his right thumbnail which refused to grow out. He wanted to fall down it and disappear.

DC Wilet's hand fell from her mouth. Far away, along her diagonal of lighter-coloured tiles, the children she had interrupted this morning now played snuggle-up-duvet, safe in their homes. Kids the murderers and murdered once had been. And, in a way, still were.

Three

Hussein Yassire slapped a set of X-ray plates against a full-length screen and dimmed the main lights. It looked like a toddler's jigsaw. Big square bits of a person standing very still, each piece easy to fit together. Detective Inspector Tilt still tasted the coffee he had left in Yassire's office. He struggled to complete the skeleton. From the X-rays the person might still be alive. Tilt's fingers folded his notepad open and replaced its rubber band.

'Why are the bones fuzzy?'

'Abrasives, John. They fog the image.' Yassire pushed his bifocals back up to the bridge of his nose. 'The technicians spent the best part of yesterday washing away the more accessible particles. Four point two kilograms in total. The fuzziness you asked about is the dust or fragments too deeply embedded into subcutaneous tissue. As a rough guide, the poorer the X-ray, the more intense the attack.'

Tilt took notes. The clarity of the hip joints merged into formless swirls around the middle of the pelvis.

'Deliberate?' he wondered out loud, felt-tip poised.

'Oh yes. The genitalia' – Yassire did not quite know how to say this – 'are missing. Not that they'd usually show on an X-ray. He's been castrated, with a sandblaster.'

Tilt drew a line across the page and then a small circle just below it, as round as he could manage. Here was a bleak inside-out world, stripped bare of virtue, where the gods of their faiths failed to provide shelter when needed. But inside the circle they were safe. He did not know how to make it bigger. It might grow smaller, be worn away to a speck, disappear into nothing. Or swallow them whole.

'Nobody should have to investigate this case, John. Nobody.'

DI Tilt turned over the page quickly. They stood close enough to embrace each other within the shadows of the X-ray screen. 'We have to investigate it,' he said, more to the page than Hussein Yassire. 'It's my job to.'

Together they worked their way back to discussing the details of the X-rays themselves. The forensic pathologist spoke to a pencil torch which cast a small arrow onto the plates. The arrow travelled down the body. The detective inspector's felt-tip followed. There was nothing critical to report. Early signs of femoral osteo-arthritis, lipping at the knee joints, otherwise a perfectly healthy man in late middle age.

'My gosh,' exclaimed Yassire with a guilty laugh. 'Those knees are back to front. I've put his legs on the wrong way round.'

Tilt laughed too. It came as a relief to make a mistake which did not matter. 'Nothing else?' he asked. 'Nothing else at all?'

'Well, he almost certainly wore shoes most of the time. It'd be odd if he didn't. Judging by the undamaged skin between his toes, he suffered from chronic low-grade athlete's foot. Why don't you see for yourself?'

Yassire flicked the X-ray screen off and Tilt followed him through the semi-darkness to gown up. Replacing the rubber band around his notebook, he noticed that he'd written the last sheet upside down. But the circle was still there, the felt-tip visible from the other side. He traced the circle precisely. He didn't want to break it.

They tied up the bows on the backs of each other's

gowns. Between the folds, Tilt felt Yassire's fingers brush his spine. Whose hands had last touched the victim's flesh while still alive?

Yassire pulled the body from the chiller. The lights over the trolley recreated the moment that Tilt pointed the sector vehicle's flashlight down the gantry steps into blasting bay six. He remembered how the plastic sheen of the incident sheet had shone straight back into his eyes. It became a strange skin which sheathed immense pain.

'Ready,' whispered Yassire without delay. He took away the cotton over-sheet and hung it inside the body chiller. Tilt recalled they otherwise freeze onto the deceased. Yassire Hussein adjusted the lights so none of the body remained in shadow. Only the soles of the feet looked human.

'Are you all right?'

'Yes. Fine,' Tilt replied. 'I'll be okay.'

His hands wanted to close the eyes of the deceased. Eyeless sockets stared straight back. He tried to comprehend the personality at the far end of the sand-blaster and failed.

They had uncovered evil.

Four

Department of Pathology
Royal Hallamshire University Hospital
Post-Mortem Report

Name: To date unknown.
Age: To date unknown; estimated 55 to 60 years.
Sex: Male.
Address: To date unknown.
Next of Kin: To date unknown.
GP details: To date unknown.
Hospital: None.   **Consultant:** None.
Mortuary Sequential No: 6584
Date & Time of Discovery: Sunday 25 January 1998, at 0349 hours.
Initial Location of Body: Reddlewood Industrial Finishers, Carrdyke Lane, S3 7GY.
Type of Post-Mortem: Complete.
Date & Place of Examination:
(i):   Tuesday 27 January, 1998, Forensic Research Centre, Sheffield.
(ii):
(iii):
(iv):
Date of Final Report: To be determined.

CAUSE OF DEATH

0a: Uncertain.

due to

0b: External Physical Means – Steel Finishing Tools.

(see Commentary & Conclusions)

EXTERNAL EXAMINATION

The body was that of a moderately well-built male in late middle-age, measuring approximately 1.78 metres (5' 10 1/4") in height and weighing approximately 65 kg (10 stone 2 lb.) This latter figure is certainly below the individual's normal weight due to significant loss of blood, other fluids and tissue immediately prior death.

Initial detail was obscured by foreign particles adhering to surface areas: these particles were removed by alcohol while the body remained in rigour (Photographs 1 & 2.)

Virtually all superficial features had been obliterated by the external physical means, namely a powerful pneumatic abrasive cleaner (Photographs 3 to 7.)

Apart from these massive cutaneous and subcutaneous injuries and trauma, all adjacent areas displayed extreme lividity, including sectors of the posterior and dorsal region protected by the seat and back of an office chair. This made visual identification of racial pigmentation far less than straight-forward. However, from intact surface tissue surviving in niches secluded from direct or indirect abrasive damage (c.f. soles of feet, webs of fingers and toes, behind the vestiges of the right ear and underneath each armpit), the individual appears to have been Euro-caucasian. Phenotypico-genetic assays may help towards confirming this.

Root follicles from the tonsure, together with pubic

samples from the ears and armpits suggest a very dark brown, virtually black hair beginning to turn white. The removal of the scalp during death means it is only possible to conject as to hair length, baldness, style and nature. Shaved follicles underneath the remains of the nose indicate the individual did not possess a moustache, (Photograph 8) however tissue damage to the faciomaxillary process entails that it cannot be said with equal certainty whether the individual did or did not wear a beard.

Intense friction burns were discovered around each ankle plus the abdomen, and immediately below the sternum (Photographs 9a, 9b, 9c and 9d.) These correlate with a blue nylon rope, (presently with the Scene of Crime Evidence Records Office) used to retain the individual to an office chair during the deployment of a steel finishing tool. Frayed strands of rope were also removed from the surface of the body as well as within bronchial passages and pulmonary fluid. These were inhaled by the victim prior death.

The frayed strands' density is greatest proximal to each side of the friction burn marks. Thus the rope burns themselves were due to the individual's movements against confinement prior to death, whereas the frayed strands themselves were caused by the steel finishing tool. It is to be noted that there are no such rope burns around either wrist, nor any matched increase in frayed strands. Nor were there any remains of fabric or leather fibres found adhering to or within the body, although a small number of flecks of paint and abraded mild steel particles were so discovered. These are presumed to be from the office chair mentioned above. A sample has been dispatched to Scene of Crime to match with the office chair.

It is not possible to pass conjecture on the colour of the individual's eyes since all tissue material had been removed, to cause the intense pitting of the underlying supra-orbital and cranial processes (Photograph 6.) Damage to the anterior teeth as far back as the second premolar is similar, although the condition of molars in all four quadrants is relatively intact. Their overall wear and status serve as the primary basis for the estimated age of late middle-age between 50 and 60. The occlusal filling of the left upper second molar appears to be a quite recent replacement where the matrix is epoxy rather than a more common mercury amalgam (Photograph 10.) This would indicate the individual could afford regular and full-cost dental treatment. Together with the lack of evidence of footwear and clothing, there were no signs of a gag, mask or adhesive tape placed across the mouth. It is not likely that all traces of such indications would be obliterated beyond examination by the steel finishing tool.

Within the natural niches formed by folds in surface tissue, between the toes lay a chronic low grade fungal infection. Its flora under examination is generically and commonly termed "athlete's foot." The skin behind the vestiges of the right ear was marginally inflamed, indicative of regular wearing of spectacles. No traces of lenses or frame have been found.

The damage to the rest of the body is relatively uniform, with between an estimated 1 mm to 5 mm of soft tissue material being removed from the original surface of the skin. Damage to the pubic area and hands is far more severe with virtually the complete removal of the testicles and penis, (Photograph 5) and all flesh from the fingers, including prints, and backs of the hands (Photograph 7.) By comparison, the palms were relatively untouched.

Microscopic examination

Aside from the fungiform organisms between the toes no other bio-medical conditions were located.

In order to assess tissue damage a regular univarate quadrate sampling strategy was deployed, where the central square centimetre in each 5 cm square was examined at low to medium powers of magnification. Although just 4% of the total surface area of the body was traversed, it also meant no portion of the body lay further than 3.5 cm from a microscopic assay (see Appendix 1 for further sampling methodology details.)

The results were singularly uniform. Typically the tissue damage is concussive, where epidermal integrity was first weakened then broken by the abrasive particles, continuing with the same momentum through the cuticle and subcuticle layers. Damage to internal organs varies according to their structure and malleability: muscles, ligaments and connective tissue remained relatively intact whereas softer organs, once exposed, (cf: lower intestine and small bowel, Photograph 4) displayed immediate degradation.

Initial examination of the pneumatic steel finishing tool shows that it was left set to fire relatively large particles at low velocities. This matches both the particles removed during cleaning the individual and the tissue damage they caused. This means of attack would expose and excite successive sets of increasingly sensitive nerve-endings within the epidermal and dermal layers. This would have caused the individual extreme distress.

Radiographic examination

4.2 kg (9 lb) of particles were removed before radiographic examination could proceed. Despite slight fogging due to residual particles and dust, the plates showed no abnormalities, clinical conditions or pathologies, apart from a minor degree of lipping and wear around both lower femoral joints. This is often indicative of osteo-arthritis, but lies within the expected range of deterioration for adults of this age. Due to the severe tissue damage around each knee it was not possible to determine if there was any chronic inflammation. Blood tests showed no traces of any anti-inflammatory or analgesic drugs: the individual may well have been unaware of this condition.

INTERNAL EXAMINATION

Cardiovascular System

The heart (497 g) was of normal size and dimensions and showed no signs of disease or abnormality.

Respiratory System

The ribs were intact. The larynx intact and unobstructed. The bronchi and trachea clear.

Where exposed, both pleural cavities were punctured by abrasive fragments. They were also filled with a mixture of abrasive particles and dust suspended in pulmonary fluid and vomit together with globules of mineral oil. This oedematous emulsion blocked over 70% of the alveoli in the right lung (865 g) and 80% in the left (902 g.) Together with the punctures this would have led to acute respiratory failure, commonly known as internal drowning.

Gastro-Intestinal System

Apart from lesions caused by the ingestion of abrasive particles, the mouth and throat were clear and uninjured.

The oesophagus and stomach were normal. The latter contained few remains of partially digested food. With the vomit found in the pleural cavities it seems the individual had not eaten for at least four to six hours before the onset of the attack.

Where undamaged, the small and large bowel were normal but empty.

The liver, (1437 g) gall bladder and pancreas were normal.

Genito-Urinary System

Both kidneys (263 g) were normal. The bladder contained virtually no urine.

Lymphoid System

The spleen (120 g) was normal.

Endocrine System

The thyroid and adrenal glands were normal.

Central Nervous System

The scalp and eyes had been pulverised and dispersed. Although pitted, the skull remained intact. Via the optical orbits the abrasive particles had also destroyed much of the frontal lobes of the brain, reducing its weight from a minimal norm of 1050 g to 835 g. In itself this may not have impaired basic control of fundamental bodily functions, but if alive, it is difficult to comprehend the sensory and intellectual damage the individual endured.

COMMENTARY

It is impractical to state an exact cause or time of death.

The final cause is likely to be one or more or all of the following factors:-

1.   External blood loss through external wounding.
2.   Respiratory failure through pulmonary punctures and oedematous fluid build-up.

3. Trauma associated with the central nervous system.
4. Psychological shock.

It is clear that death was far from instantaneous. At the velocities the abrasives were fired at the body, it would have taken many minutes, if not an hour or more to inflict damage to the skin sufficient to allow an apposite loss of blood. This finding is backed by the build-up of pulmonary fluid: although some might have been post-mortem, the observed blocking of alveoli could only occur over a significant period of time prior to death. Each of these arguments alone is sufficient to provide a length of attack well in excess of forty-five minutes. An upper limit is more difficult to locate. However both arguments are supported by the elimination of virtually all urine and faeces. For all these processes to transpire, the individual remained alive for upwards of two hours during the attack – almost regardless of any trauma to the central nervous system or psychological shock.

By this time his assailants might also have encountered difficulties in the determination of life or death, yet little if any abrasive damage can be ascribed to the time after death. This may mean that the individual was still left alive at the end of the attack.

In summation, the individual endured an attack by low velocity abrasive particles between 45 and 180 minutes, resulting in death then, or shortly thereafter. From the evidence available the attack most probably lasted around 120 minutes.*

Although absence of evidence is not necessarily evidence of absence, the individual appears to have been entirely naked throughout the attack. His legs and upper body were tied to a chair but his arms and head were free to move without restraint. The attack was most intense around the pelvis, the head and the back of the hands. This is most simply explained by the individual alternately attempting to protect his face or his genitalia with his hands. This being the case, it entails the individual was castrated alive. Furthermore, the extreme damage to both eye sockets, then the frontal lobes of the brain would only have occurred after the individual became incapable of raising his arms. He remained fully conscious and aware until then.

The body was discovered just before four a.m., with a preliminary forensic examination following ten hours later. Its condition then would place the attack somewhere after eight o'clock the evening beforehand through to three the next morning.

CONCLUSIONS

Post-mortem examination demonstrates that death occurred through traumatic damage inflicted by abrasive particles from a steel-finishing tool deliberately fired by an unknown party between 2000 hrs Saturday 24 January and 0300 hrs Sunday 25 January, 1998.

Post-mortem examination failed to provide any clear evidence to identify the deceased, or his assailants.

Post-mortem examination indicated the deceased was in sound physical health immediately prior the attack.

* Experimental replication could serve to narrow the range of time estimates. This would entail the deployment of a similar pneumatic steel finishing tool on appropriate animal flesh, if necessary.

Hussein Yassire scrolled back to the start of the report to check through it once more. He added frayed rope strands to the oil globules and vomit in the oedematous emulsion that filled the lungs, but decided against removing psychological shock as a fatal factor.

In the medical world no one dies from pain. He pressed the print button.

Five

Detective Chief Inspector Bill Naylor could not reach across to switch off the radio alarm. He was already up, sitting on the toilet in agony. Piles ran in the family, he told himself. Spikes of pain speared his stomach and disappeared from where they came. Tenderly he wiped his own backside and pulled the lever. The cistern reverberated with the sound of cars teasing their way through the snow. Sheffield always made a mess of snow. The gritter lorries went on strike or Sheff FM said leave work early so the early leavers jammed the gritter lorries in their depots, even if they weren't on strike. No point rushing in today; it would only make matters worse. He ran a tap until the water felt hot enough for a shave, then brushed his teeth instead. The radio switched itself off.

Bill Naylor lived on his own. All down to shiftwork. Everyone agreed the job took you away from the family: many found this an attraction. For years he had watched their children grow up alongside the Leylandii conifers at the far end of their garden. His wife's brother had planted them the summer they moved in, more or less a generation ago. They never quite got round to having the brother-in-law build the extension they had agreed to before exchange of contracts. Instead the kids, then his wife left him, to look after the Leylandii by himself.

Today they reached the gutter line of the house and left

the garden in perpetual shade. He preferred his life now to how it was then. Once he got over the loss of familiarity he found himself free to do more or less what he liked at home. Which was little except drink. Not too much; he kept himself pretty fit, all in all, just a bit paunchy and the occasional bout of flu or what his father had called the collywobbles. It didn't seem to trouble him; he could look after himself. Except the piles. 'Bloody haemorrhoids,' he swore out loud. They were starting to make a real arse out of his life.

After walking her grandchildren to school, Mrs Eccles came to clean twice a week. He put his shopping list with three ten pound notes by the sink. Eight years had passed with her ironing out the same old creases and collecting up the next set of empties. She would have asked whether she ought to buy them as well, but Mr Naylor still called her Mrs Eccles, never Grace. Even down to the label stuck to the hurriedly wrapped Christmas present of inexpensive sherry left with her wages beside the sink. He did not know her Christian name. Bill Naylor went to work without a shave, and without quite knowing why.

When he arrived, he knew he had to see DI Tilt. He and his flu had forced Tilt into the empty building to process the recovery, removal and dissection of the remains. He needed to pick up the pieces before it was too late. He tried to avoid eye-contact as he entered the section office. His flu had left him feeling hungover for nearly a week. DCI Naylor rubbed the jowl line below his chin before realizing he hadn't shaved.

Tilt handed over the papers without a word. Through the frosted glass of the office divider he watched a female shape pass their DCI in the corridor. DC Wilet wasn't due in this morning.

'Hello, sir. Magistrate's been put back with the snow till this afternoon,' she explained.

Tilt nodded. 'Do you want to try getting hold of Detective Superintendent Singleterry? We need him here for the case conference.'

He did not need to say anything more.

Inside his own office Detective Chief Inspector Naylor wished he had eaten breakfast. Hunger precipitated the urge to drink; it was a hard three hours before he could sensibly leave for lunch. Somehow he'd manage, he always had. Lips paused at the mistyped words of the report of crime sheet. He wasn't sure how to react to the Reddlewood case. There wasn't enough down on paper. The ROC contained less data than Mrs Eccles's shopping list: no names; no witnesses; no arrests; not much to go on – typos weren't much use as facts.

Facts. Naylor went through them again.

Some silly sods had sandblasted some other stupid sod to death. So what? These things happen, like snow or haemorrhoids. Nasty things. That's what the police are there for. To put an end to it all, to stop what's wrong with the world. That's why we need things on paper, Naylor thought, written down in black and white. Each detail, to force the Crown Prosecution Service to take it to court, to make sure the half-arsed twats who sit on the bench or jury really do nail the sodding bastards who cause all this paperwork in the first place. Facts on paper mean results.

While others swore and seethed at their monotony, DCI Naylor survived through police forms and procedures. They helped him feel in control – like cigarettes. Naylor's hand felt for his packet. After he cleared his desk he would take his break in the designated smoking area down the corridor.

Paperwork: the power in an officer's notebook, the custody desk's charge sheet. Naylor folded and slipped each piece of paper into its rightful place inside the right cardboard file (according to regulation procedure), to produce not just a report, but a three-dimensional picture. Reality on paper. An image the simplest juror would take to be true beyond all reasonable doubt. Guilty as proven. From incident sheets to court statement, results meant paperwork. Words, not deeds, obtained convictions.

Not that Naylor did everything by the book, what copper did? But he left no loose ends. He made sure he physically cleared his desk at the end of each day. He kept his office bare. Rank and surname etched onto a twelve-year-old bare aluminium plate screwed to a blank door provided the only evidence for his existence.

The section needed a good case. Not a strong one, still less open and shut. Naylor had been in plainclothes for too long not to act before things grew a little too quiet just a little too often. The signs were there: special operations had gone off half-cock; local initiatives become routine; absenteeism, his own included, was creeping up; a couple of dents in pool cars; snide smiles from other DCIs. They needed a good case. A case which became an investigation, not necessarily major. No, probably not major, but big enough for them to handle. Their section's clear-up rate invariably rose just before each and every review. Naylor made sure it did, by feeding the system the right paperwork at the right time. Paperwork meant results. Everyone else did it too; Naylor did it better than most. In his book paperwork was results.

This was a good case, the case every plod and plonk spooned into their canteen cuppa as assistant chief constables bragged across force boundaries. It secured a section's future. They did not need to solve this case, certainly not quickly. They only needed to be seen to be busy investigating it. This was hardly difficult to manage. The Reddlewood investigation became an each-way bet, a banker of a result. On his way out Naylor told one of the civilians to pass the message on that he would meet the team after lunch. He had earned himself a drink today.

Detective Superintendent Jack Singleterry sat himself behind Naylor's empty desk, his long legs squeezed in at an angle. They had started probationary training near enough the same day thirty-odd years ago: 1964. Peter Swan and 'Bronco' Layne had been done for throwing Wednesday's last few games of the season. They did time. Singleterry lit a cigarette. Station policy prohibited smoking in your own office or place of work; it didn't say anything about other people's. He looked for an ashtray, a polystyrene cup, a picture of a loved one, something in the bin. Nothing.

As smoke swirled into his lungs he found himself back at the Owls' first home game the next season – 'Jack, it's not the same without Swanny and Bronco' – and for a brief serrated moment he and Billy Naylor had felt guilty. Their uniforms had locked up their heroes. Not simply heroes. Swanny and Bronco were on cigarette cards – they were gods. The moment shattered once the Leppings Lane end hurled abuse at their uniforms. 'Half-time,' said their sergeant, 'tell us who you want sorting. Three lines in book.'

Three thousand arrests later and what did Billy Naylor have? No family, no future, no framed photograph on his desk, no commendations, never mind medals in its drawers. Detective Superintendent Singleterry gained success by making sure he was far too dangerous to cross. He flicked his cigarette ash onto his colleague's floor. He knew he had little more than Naylor, except power. He didn't feel sorry for him either. The skiving half-fit bastard was still in the pub supping, while he'd been stuck in snow over the Snake Pass, no one getting through to him about this shit-headed murder they had landed on his desk. No, not his desk. Naylor's. That was where it belonged.

When he saw his own office door ajar Naylor knew what to expect. His tongue comforted itself against a large strong mint as he waited for Singleterry to get up from his desk. Singleterry remained seated, his short white head of hair not moving an inch. He did not look up.

'Had it with waiting, Bill. Up to here. Five fucking hours on Snake, no one says what's off and no one's waiting for me when I get back. Fuck it, Bill, or some bastard upstairs will sodding well stick you.'

Bill nodded. When they had started in the force together he used to look after Singleterry. Kept him out of trouble whenever his surly contempt of procedure might unsettle their superiors. He smoothed out the rough edges in an investigation, explained away any visible marks left on a suspect on return to custody. He was like Mrs Eccles; he kept Jack Singleterry's world tidy for him. He knew the favour would never be returned. Singleterry remained seated and lit another cigarette.

'Get the other dossers in here.'

Ten minutes later Detective Inspector Tilt watched Detective Superintendent Singleterry thumb through a set of Polaroids from scene of crime. They could be someone else's holiday snaps for all the attention he gave them.

'Get on with it, inspector. We haven't got all fucking day, have we?'

DI Tilt repeated details he had already reported to the DCI yesterday. They were down on paper beneath the Polaroids on Naylor's desk. Senior officers complained without fail and at length of never having the time to read the reports they ordered their junior officers to write.

Singleterry never read or listened to anything if it could be helped; it made life simpler. He went back to his cigarette.

Bill Naylor smiled a little while adjusting the waistband of his trousers. He knew the best reports were those which were never read, just accepted. It was the easiest way to secure a conviction. They were already starting to bury the paperwork.

'We've located the receivers, sir,' Tilt added. 'A company based near Reading. According to their records the last workers were laid off around the middle of November. A couple of men may have come in later for a couple of days for maintenance. We're checking them first, of course. The services were about to be disconnected, pending the sale of disposable assets. The receivers did express a concern that our investigation does not unduly interfere –'

'Did they? You tell them that when we nail these murdering bastards, their briefs'll doubtless persuade the judge to dole out a shitload of community service to clean up their stinking disposable assets.' Like many other policemen, Singleterry believed prison worked but the judicial system didn't. Police investigations determined guilt because they had the facts, because they got their sodding hands dirty. Singleterry's own bony fingers spread out the Polaroids, flattened them against Naylor's desk. Then he started to arrange them in an odd game of patience, only to stop when he couldn't see a solution or the rules to this macabre activity. He dropped his cigarette butt onto the floor to flatten it with an unnecessarily heavy stamp. The Polaroids' chilled sheen of sandblasted bone and flesh were harder to put out.

'At least they rule out suicide.' Jack Singleterry never really bothered to feel anything. His tone of voice failed to indicate whether he expected his officers to laugh. They kept quiet, like his missus. One smack, premeditated but without reason straight after their honeymoon had kept her from answering back for the rest of their marriage. He still hit her every now and then because he enjoyed giving her a cold hard slap. It turned him on. He roughly shuffled the photographs and shoved them into the bottom drawer of Naylor's desk. 'Crap for Identikit. Shame you were poorly, Bill. Missed all the fun.'

John Tilt found it difficult to listen. He was tired, but not that tired. His ears kept picking up sounds outside the room. Boots along the corridor, a gritter lorry grumbling down the street, the distant ringing of phones left unanswered. A swish of grit smacked the tarred cobbles below but he heard the incident sheet brush over torn flesh – swish. Tilt tried to reconcile these sounds with an update of last month's budget headings. The cost of investigation did little to quell the noise of murder. It only seemed to make it easier to listen elsewhere.

Singleterry wanted Naylor to explain how nowhere near enough cash lay in the reserves to extend hours. In Tilt's office beforehand everyone had accepted that this meant they'd have to call in the Serious Crime Squad from Leeds. City Division had stretched themselves executing a fake goods initiative alongside trading standards officers in the run-up to Christmas. They had embarrassed everyone into the bargain: half the expensive toiletries most coppers had bought their women and half the official soccer strips they'd bought their lads weren't – genuine, that is. They'd wrapped them up and stuck them under their Christmas trees all the same. If the law couldn't tell the difference, who else would?

'Leave you lot alone for five minutes,' Singleterry interrupted, 'and uniform piss all over us.' He nearly laughed. The left-overs remaining in the current financial year had helped fund Operation Blue Flush. Late one night uniform had collared a drunk pissing next to the council leader's official car, in front of the council leader and the divisional commander. Each conveniently forgot they had done much the same in their own youth. 'A free democracy cannot tolerate individuals urinating in shop doorways and down dark alleys,' the council leader wrote in his newspaper column. 'Sheffield City deserves better.' The council leader was right, of course, but he should have read the rest of the paper. 'They've shut all the public toilets,' the culprit told the magistrates, 'and I voted for the bastard.' More fool him, agreed the bench, who in a million years would never have voted for the bastard. They doubled their original sentence for contempt of court. Operation Blue Flush was the divisional commander's answer. Highly trained officers lay in wait throughout the night to catch perpetrators in the very act of emptying their bladders onto city streets. They arrested a teacher, a male nurse and two off-duty special constables. The rest were too quick on their feet to be apprehended. Blue Flush let plainclothes take the piss out of uniform.

'You've stuffed overtime. What's left?' Singleterry ignored DCI Naylor. 'Ashurst?'

'I'm not sure, sir,' replied the sergeant from operational resources. 'Local initiatives? Burglary's down and snow usually hits car thieves.'

'Tilt.'

'It is your decision, sir. However, I really feel we just do not have the resources to conduct this investigation as we would want.' Tilt watched Singleterry stare past the relief's notes and tried to stop digging a hole before Singleterry buried him in it. 'It may be better to consider alternative strategies, sir. The information is insufficient –'

'Inspector, the information is all we've got.'

'I appreciate that, sir.'

'Then shut the hell up, inspector. Crime doesn't wait for "alternative strategies". Why should we?'

John Tilt knew it was hopeless to attempt to talk, never mind argue with Singleterry. His fists clenched all the same. It hadn't stopped him from trying.

'Naylor.'

Tilt winced as Naylor turned pale. He knew that Naylor

and Singleterry had worked their way up the ranks together. When Tilt had first requested a transfer from operations to training nine years ago, they were still both chief inspectors: Bill and Jack, two men who were equals, a team. Singleterry was a ruthless interrogator. He possessed the cold talent to find the exact act to dismember a suspect's self-esteem. Now he did the same to his colleagues. For him to address Naylor by his surname from Naylor's own desk in front of junior officers could hardly be more humiliating. Both men knew it.

'I think I'd have to agree with Sergeant Ashurst, sir.' What else could the chief inspector say? He felt abandoned, his body bulk squeezed into nothing – far less than the space behind the bare metal nameplate screwed to his door. This lunchtime it had seemed large enough to hide inside for ever. 'Possibly reduce our active caseload as a temporary measure?'

'Let's do both. Cut local initiatives and active caseload,' stated Singleterry, ready to leave. 'I want this murder and I want it investigated by us. Have the new work schedules on Chief Inspector Naylor's desk by this evening. That's all.'

It was simple to switch resources, there were so few to switch. Singleterry remained in charge of the investigation, with Naylor responsible for day-to-day operations. He'd co-ordinate two teams. One to examine material evidence, the other to chase leads and interrogate witnesses or suspects.

DC Wilet mentioned something to DI Tilt and DS Ashurst which DCI Naylor did not quite catch. She took her coat and left. It didn't seem important.

They waited for Naylor to decide who would lead each team. Naylor waited for someone else to speak. No one did. Two minutes later the three men started to grin sheepishly at one another in the confused silence.

Naylor had forgotten where they had got to. He felt ill trying to remember – Jack Singleterry had been a friend. It hurt. Why come to work? Not to be hurt. He wished he had stayed at home. 'Find us some tea, love,' he eventually said. 'Oh, she's gone. Must be this flu.'

'Yes, sir,' replied Ashurst, in a tone as though their DCI had made a staggering insight. Naylor still looked lost: Ashurst had to continue, lead the way. 'Magistrates' Court, sir. Postponed until this afternoon. Shall I phone down to the canteen?'

'Canteen? Why?'

'For tea, sir. You said you wanted tea.'

'Tea?' echoed the DCI. 'No, we're too busy.' Bill Naylor wanted to go home and lie down with a drink and something inert on TV. He daren't move in case his piles started up again. Suddenly it hurt far too much to feel anything else. 'Sergeant Ashurst – Neil, no, Nick.'

'It is Neil, sir. Right first time.'

'I want you to work alongside me. Inspector Tilt, may we leave you to handle material evidence?'

'By all means, sir.'

'Gives continuity. You're the initiating officer.'

'Yes, sir.'

'Having flagged it up with the super.'

'Yes, sir.'

They waited for the DCI to stop regurgitating dead information. Tilt listened to the flatness in Naylor's voice: alcohol impairs performance. Tilt had heard it his first afternoon back at operations. As soon as he had, he tried to pretend he hadn't. What else could he do? Naylor so utterly failed to pick up a medley of hints that Tilt didn't know if Naylor was in complete denial or ignorance of his condition. Did he even know he'd come to work unshaven? Did he care? Did it matter? Any official action would bury the remains of both their careers. What good would that do? The force accepted drunk coppers so long as they did their duty. Which included loyalty and trust, not grassing up other coppers. 'A cover-up,' Tilt's wife had said when he finally got home late last Sunday night, yet Tilt had kept quiet because he didn't want to talk about it. Neither did she. Not flu at all, just a cover-up.

A sense of duty drove Naylor to records. He already knew who he and Jack would suspect. Sorry, not Jack, he forced himself to confess. Detective Superintendent Singleterry to you, Naylor. You can't call him Jack again, not after thirty-odd years of service together.

Naylor laid the record cards out more or less how his superior had placed the Polaroids across his desk. He picked out a few names, remembered how they had broken them, ripped out their confessions, whatever the rules. Extort, bargain, frighten. Words that were never heard or spoken were the quickest way to secure a conviction, but beating them out of a suspect seemed to give Jack – no, the detective superintendent – an instant hit. Bill Naylor had been the nasty one, Jack Singleterry cruelty itself. Perhaps he was missing it, perhaps it explained why he was starting to beat up on his colleagues. It hurt.

Some time later the records clerk walked over to Naylor's table, where his head had slumped down over the record cards. The clerk had to shake the DCI's shoulders several times quite firmly before he opened his eyes, focused and pulled himself to. They had to leave, it was dark outside, the records office was closing. Naylor had forgotten the names he'd picked out. His hands felt his pockets, for his cigarettes, car keys; his bare metal nameplate. His identity. Time to go; everyone else had, Jack Singleterry a long time ago. He had thrown Bill Naylor away like an empty packet of cigarettes.

*

In the section office they had expected their DCI to complete the new work schedules, only he had rung through to tell them to write up the details. He'd be in records; he'd said he couldn't think straight in his own office. No one had disagreed; he was probably too soused to think straight anywhere.

Ten minutes after finishing, Tilt gave up ringing for a copy typist and walked down to discover all civilian staff were excused duty due to 'Ambient Weather Deterioration'.

'You mean it's snowing.'

'If you say so, sir,' said the desk sergeant. 'But it's not as bad as Derbyshire.'

The DI peered through the frosted door to reception. Blurred sodden figures stood and sat between the main entrance and a toughened glass security screen. Members of the public, you and I, urging someone to take action. Answer a buzzer which never really works.

'No,' Tilt said to himself, 'I don't suppose it is.'

Nothing in City Division was ever as bad as Derbyshire.

No one had thought to tell them about the empty typing pool. They'd have to type up the schedules too. The last to leave the office, Tilt went downstairs and waited for the photocopier to warm up. The snow started to thicken against the copier room windows. He reversed the order of the report, last sheet first to make it easier to sort out the copies, except they came out squint. There seemed to be something inside the machine, which had somehow managed to slip past the broken buzzer and the toughened glass security screen at the main entrance. Tilt opened the copier front and crouched down. Everything looked fine, felt warm. At the second time of asking it worked well enough; perhaps it was how he had fed in the originals. Before leaving for home he remembered to turn off the lights in the room and their section office, but like most police officers he also forgot to switch off the photocopier.

*

A shopping list with three ten pound notes lay untouched next to the kitchen sink. The phone rang and Sheff FM chattered away to itself upstairs, bad news about a business airport. Bill Naylor hardly listened. Who gave a flying fuck about business airports? Sheffield wasn't that sort of place. The noise stopped and two minutes later it started again; he must have pressed the snooze button this morning.

Mrs Eccles redialled his number. She wanted to explain to Mr Naylor how she had to while away the whole day with her grandchildren in the house, what with the snow and the schools closed and all. She'd come again in the morning, if that were all right with Mr Naylor. Bill Naylor let the phone ring. They could wait, as he had waited inside records tonight. Grace Eccles gave up.

The phone stopped ringing. The Sheffield he and Jack Singleterry understood was a closed world. No one came in, no one left, except to return. The pain of loneliness tore at his guts.

Six

The snow had gone by the end of the week. From a derelict foundry opposite, Ruth Wilet watched the cobblestones in Reddlewood's yard. Through her personal stereo she heard but hardly listened to Sheff FM's timecheck. She didn't want to know there were a further six hours to the end of her shift. Dead engine oil darkened the cobbles. 'Don't fret yourself, girl,' Detective Superintendent Singleterry had ordered. 'Police radios always work, don't they?' They hadn't at Hillsborough and everyone in the force knew it.

DC Wilet let her bird-watching binoculars focus once more onto the castings left in the yard. She had wanted to visit the Dark Peak with her partner, mountain-bike up from Ladybower Reservoir to the Stirrings through the damp early morning mist that cleaned the hillsides, freshened its air. They'd stand still enough to hear fledgling game birds scurry from their breath, the quick patter of beaks, feet and ruffled feathers. Then silence as their breath became two tongues of mist, then one. Pure empty silence, at ease with itself – but she wasn't there. Other creatures were harder to disturb within her Dark Peak imagination. Swathes of rock-cold bracken merged together into a ridge of grey-green scales, a skin filmed with moisture; coarse and reptilian. In her mind a huge slumbering beast which reeked of stagnant earth. She

51

didn't want to know where it had come from. She focused back to the castings.

She was on placement, she could hardly say no to her detective superintendent. 'Customs and Excise need back-up,' he had announced, bleak eyes patrolling the room as he kept his head still. Why was Singleterry pulling in outsiders when he'd wanted to keep the case to himself? There had to be a reason, a devious reason. They all knew the super was up to something, and no one had dared say a word.

Ruth Wilet realized she could have excused herself long before then; male coppers expected women to powder their noses every five minutes. She had never powdered her nose in her life. There were no toilets left in this building; the room stank from where men, policemen, had stood in a corner and pissed. So much for Operation Blue Flush.

At the next weather report she'd check the signal on her mobile, see the warmth of her partner's number in its LED display. She had kept quiet about her in the station canteen, told them she had a boyfriend instead. They'd have thought her a girlie if she didn't have a man. Girlies were plonks who couldn't cope on their own, who couldn't cope with men, but lezzies were an unnatural half-species. No mobile phone on earth could help her cope with policemen. She had to visit the Dark Peak to banish the stench of their city; the LED display inside her outdoor gear kept her from freezing.

It began to rain hard. Through her binoculars she thought she saw the tracks of a small animal cross the cobbles. She completed her tally of castings in the yard of the empty building.

Last Thursday the detective super had kept them waiting for over twenty minutes. He made no apology as he stood between them and the door. 'Fatwah still can't say how the bastard died, never mind who the fuck the bastard is.'

Singleterry thumped Naylor's desk with the post-mortem report. 'It's fucking obvious how he died.' Everyone else in the room clamped their mouths shut as their detective superintendent decided who to fix with his eyes. 'They blasted his bollocks to buggery then blew out his brains.' DI Tilt stared straight back. Singleterry relished the contest. He couldn't see how a creeping Jesus like Tilt was ever allowed to become a copper in the first place. 'This post mortem's about as much use as your dick. Generally speaking.'

Wilet noticed DI Tilt's fist tighten while he attempted to answer. 'We discussed Yassire's findings earlier, sir. How the identity of the victim had been deliberately obliterated.'

'I am aware of the facts, inspector.'

'Yes, sir. It would appear to match scene of crime's lack of associated fingerprints.'

Apart from the bootmarks, visor scraps and a dozen small machine-cut squares of flimsy polythene, the only practical forensics SOCO had turned up were fingerprints all over the machinery. A set matched a local burglar. They'd rushed to bring him in but were stopped by his broken arm. Their prime suspect had spent the night of the murder waiting in casualty for the plaster cast now slung beneath an empty sweatshirt sleeve. 'Reddlewood's fired him while Christmas,' his woman explained. 'We still haven't seen redundancy money.' She hadn't. He'd kept it for a flutter with a woman he visited under the pretence of physiotherapy outpatients. 'Benefit don't stretch to a smoke.'

DCI Naylor had ignored her attempts to cadge a cigarette. They all knew her man had fallen fifteen feet breaking and entering into a farmhouse near Hathersage: people seldom install burglar alarms upstairs. 'Fell off ladder,' he told the two officers. 'Cleaning windows.' His woman had pushed him into burgling again. Two toddlers in stale pyjamas stared in silence at a worn-out *Thomas the Tank Engine* video, stale thumbs in mouths. DCI Naylor felt sorry for the kids, DC Wilet for the woman.

She watched Singleterry take a step forward, towards Tilt. 'You were about to tell us that this is the work of professional criminals, inspector. To be exact, four pairs of boots plan to torture then execute their victim, then disappear in a single vehicle, leaving just tyre marks behind in the snow, which your little girlie here recorded for us. Have I missed something?'

'You've not missed anything.' They stood eye to eye. 'It's DC Wilet, sir.'

'Quite right, inspector, my apologies. DC Wilet, it must be reassuring to have a superior officer with your interests so much to heart. Quite a big girlie, aren't we, inspector?'

Ruth Wilet and Jack Singleterry saw Tilt's face redden, then grow white as he forced himself to be calm.

'Well, inspector?'

'Sir.' Neck muscles still pushed against shirt collar. 'We have been considering implications.'

'Really. Implications?'

'Yes, sir. The murderers set out to obscure their victim's identity, but only from us, the police. Nobody else. Otherwise why leave the body behind? They wanted it to be found.'

'Go on.' Jack Singleterry smiled. His eyes narrowed with the effort. 'Do go on.'

DI Tilt found it difficult to. No one likes being interrogated, and it was more Naylor's theory in the first place. Tilt knew they didn't rate him as a detective, a thief-taker. He never had himself. He had always wanted to prevent crime, not just catch criminals.

'There has to be a reason, sir. It's far safer to dispose of the body altogether, as far as possible from the scene of the crime. Throw it into the river, bury it for ever. Instead they leave it behind to be discovered, not by us, sir, but by people who knew the victim. As the relief inspector put it, they must've been sending a message to them. If you've read their report, SOCO reckon the polythene squares are the backs to Polaroid film. The perpetrators may have sent them a picture. To someone, a group, a gang who'd miss seeing the victim alive. A warning perhaps, sir, or a threat. They expected someone else to find the body. Not us. They left the body behind quite deliberately. They wanted to get a reaction.'

'Very good, inspector. Very good indeed. Uniform just chances to find it following tyre tracks in the snow. No prints on polythene squares, mind. That would be damning, wouldn't it?'

Singleterry walked past them to the window as though they did not exist. He spoke slowly and buried his dialect. Now was as good a time as any to spring his little surprise.

'And if the body is a message, we would expect someone to come along and pick it up, wouldn't we? And we would dearly love to know just who those someones were. You never know, with a bit of luck they might just lead us right back to the murderers, the people who we are meant to be looking for. Are you still with me? Which means we should have been watching the site around the fucking clock, doesn't it?'

Naylor stared down at the post-mortem report. Tilt and Wilet found themselves exchanging a hurried glance. Singleterry lit a cigarette.

'Well, say something then. Like: "Oh dear, how remiss of us, superintendent." Perhaps I should have told you that as from today I've arranged for surveillance of Carrdyke Lane by Customs and Excise. I'm afraid I let them believe that we have evidence which points to this killing being part of a turf war, involving at least one major drugs firm. They're quite sold on the idea, so please don't disabuse them of this slight deception, will you, gentlemen? And I think that also answers your next question, Detective Inspector Tilt. The one you are still too scared to ask about calling in the Serious Crime Squad from Leeds. We can fuck up perfectly well on our own, thank you very much. Now, I'd like to help DCI Naylor interrogate potential suspects – if that's all right by you, Bill. Oh yes, Customs and Excise need back-up.'

Between the usual Sunday traffic hold-ups around Meadowhall, Sheff FM reminded listeners that the body taken from the River Don behind the old British Steel Carrdyke Works remained unidentified. Police were appealing for witnesses with any further information. Detective Superintendent Singleterry told FM Crime that this would help them trace the deceased's close relatives. 'Someone out there,' he said, 'is doubtlessly missing a loved one.' DC Wilet stopped listening. She knew the police were lying, not just about the location of the body, but to each other, to Customs and Excise, to whoever listened. A non-existent story to eke out a non-existent budget. If DI Tilt couldn't start to question the lies and deceit, more fool her if she dared try.

DC Wilet decided to switch off Sheff FM but listened to Sheffield instead. She needed something to take her mind off the task of finding a safe place to pee. She raised her binoculars and saw herself a week ago, white gloves clutching a notebook as rust from the gantry rail stained its damp pale pages, her toes half-frozen in the snow. If it had not fallen, the two local beat officers would have driven straight past. The body would still be there right now. There was no safe place to pee.

A small ordinary van drove past slowly. Its driver tried to stop mumbling to himself.

*

Harry Noyes stopped digging out an old vegetable bed, to watch a dark saloon park halfway down Hangingwater Lane. He hated gardening. Definitely plainclothes: too clean, too anonymous a car to be anything else. Probably just a burglary. But instead of crossing the road to one of the quiet semis, two overcoated officers squeezed through the broken gate which led to the allotments and started to clamber up the path towards where Harry was standing. He ducked his head. He knew them from a long way back. He believed those times were over. What did they want from him? What were they after now?

'Hello there, Harry,' began Bill Naylor. 'Jack and I here have a few questions.'

'Bet you have,' Harry replied, not looking up.

'Didn't know you liked gardening.'

'I don't. Were that one of your questions?'

'No. But we didn't reckon your Beryl. She said you were out here, gardening.'

'She said that? You have to do something, inspector.'

'Indeed you do. By the way, it's chief inspector, Harry. And Mr Singleterry here is a superintendent.'

Harry stared at them. 'You're still –'

'What?' Singleterry demanded. 'My pencil's nice and sharp so I can write it down in my notebook.'

'Welcome to ask a few questions,' replied Harry, thrusting the spade deep into the tilth. He had nothing left to hide, which made him feel vulnerable, naked. No one else was out working on the allotments.

'Keep digging,' continued Singleterry. 'We wouldn't want you to get stiff and cold, would we?'

Harold Noyes felt like taking the spade and splitting Singleterry's head in two. Instead he kept digging, burying plants and weeds alike under the upturned earth. He didn't know what else to do. His boot slid off the spade as its blade hit a piece of old bottle. He rubbed his shin through two layers of old trousers, could almost feel the blood seep onto his gloved fingers. He looked halfway up towards Mr Naylor.

'Sorry,' said the DCI, and they both knew they were talking about an accident long ago. 'Harry, what's with allotment if you don't like gardening?'

'It isn't mine, Mr Naylor. It's – do you mind if we don't talk about it?'

'All right, Harry. After all, you can hardly steal an allotment, can you?'

Harry shrugged his shoulders and resumed digging, head down.

'How long did you do at Strangeways?' Singleterry asked.

'Ten year, and it were Leicester. You should know, you put me there.'

'I did? Ten year, lovely gardens there and you still don't like gardening. Perhaps you should do some more. You see, I've heard you're finding retirement difficult to cope with. You've been itching to get back to work, find a little job somewhere or the other.'

'Don't mind retirement, inspector – superintendent. It's gardening I don't like, and having to explain –'

'In fact this little job's right up your street, Harry. Wouldn't you say so, chief inspector? When we heard about it, we said to ourselves, Harry Noyes, definitely Harry Noyes. Didn't know he took pictures, though.'

'What are you on about? I am retired, superintendent.'

'Shame he's retired, we said, real shame,' continued Singleterry. 'When he were working, we said to ourselves, he'd kill for a job like this. Kill.'

Harold Noyes kept his head down digging. Singleterry squeezed everything you said until it came out the way he wanted it to come out. His shin started to hurt.

'I'd stop digging if I were you,' Singleterry advised. 'Unless you want to excavate path.'

They watched him shove the spade back into the earth. Bill Naylor wondered if he should do something about his own garden before the neighbours again started to say things behind his back loud enough for him to overhear. It was still far too cold, even to listen.

'Excuse me, Chief Inspector Naylor. I wonder if you have a spare pencil about your person. Mine seems to have broken. A nice sharp pencil.'

Singleterry heard his suspect try to breathe deeply through his nose and smiled. Harold Noyes had been found guilty and was duly sent down for ten years with good behaviour, but not for the crimes he had committed. Singleterry and Naylor didn't have a clue about them. Instead they had kept at him until his solicitor had to excuse himself to go to the toilet. Singleterry sharpened his pencil, then leant across the table to grab Noyes' hair to shove the pencil up each of his nostrils. Long before the solicitor returned, Harry Noyes had stopped screaming. 'Your client's had a bit of nosebleed, I'm afraid. DS Naylor's gone to fetch first aid tin.'

Harry Noyes would just as easily have done much the same to Singleterry had their positions been reversed. They all knew that. The Noyes boys voted Tory because Reginald Maudling opened mile after mile of motorway. As wagons left rail for road they became the first in the north to exploit their isolation. The Noyes boys controlled all the cigarettes, spirits, perfume, televisions that fell off the backs of lorries just off the M1 between Woodhall and Wooley Edge Services. They left the Great Train Robbery behind as a magnificent anachronism.

They took the money and ran before sealed containers and CB radios made it too risky a trade by half. Harry and Charlie bought a couple of the clubs where they had sold on the cheap cigarettes and spirits. Harry looked after the business, Charlie the problems. Harry was the eldest.

While he did time at Leicester and without Freddie to help, Charlie found the business too much of a problem on his own. He had started to do odd things like ban green pullovers and introduce topless bingo. Harry saw the drug dealing inside Leicester and instructed the family's solicitor to sell up, legitimately. A week later Beryl visited her husband in prison for the first time in eight years. She had always wanted her Harold to be straight, easy to control.

Now Harry looked at the spade and the upturned earth. There was nothing left to hide. 'Talk to my wife, superintendent. Ask Beryl. I leave her to watch after our interests now.'

'We did,' lied Singleterry. 'She's just as keen as ourselves to know what you've been up to.' They both knew it didn't matter an inch if Singleterry had lied. 'We could all go back together, have a cup of tea and ask her again. Harry, I'd like that cup of tea.'

Harry rubbed both sides of his nose. Singleterry was a diabolical bastard. If he wasn't a copper, he'd have been found dead years ago. Charlie had wanted him buried when Harry moved to Leicester. He had wanted to kill a policeman ever since Freddie died. Harry said no. 'You've three kids you love, Charlie. If you kill that fucking bastard, you'll have every fucking policeman in South Yorkshire looking to nail you and your kids, who you'll never ever fucking see again. Do you hate Singleterry more than you love your kids?' Charlie looked at his elder brother with anger, attempting to buckle the back of this dilemma. Harry let Charlie hit him. Square on the jaw with all the muscle his body had in store for Singleterry. The decision was made.

Harry stared at the superintendent's black shiny lace-ups on the edge of the path. I saved your life, he thought. Charlie would've murdered you. No doubt about it, you lucky fucking bastard.

'Most of these allotments seem unused, Bill.' Singleterry ignored Noyes completely. 'Seems a shame, all that hard work going to waste. I used to sit in those classrooms up there as a kid. Each of these allotments were kept immaculate. Pretty little huts and sheds too, some had stoves inside. They say people passed them on behind council's back, otherwise you'd spend a lifetime on waiting list. Easy for some, isn't it? All gone now, of course. Kids come here to sniff glue and shag themselves silly in sheds they've yet to smash. You'd have thought schools'd encourage them to keep allotments, as part of biology or civic duty or something, wouldn't you, right here on their doorstep? But then I got blackboard duster round my fucking ear for looking out of that fucking window. Where were you and Charlie last Saturday night?'

'Home, with Beryl. Ask her, 'cos you don't believe me. Charlie and I'd have been here except for weather. He were probably at Anna's.'

'Anna?'

'Anna Grice. His daughter Anna. He spends weekend at hers.'

'Right. So neither of you were anywhere near Carrdyke Lane.'

'Ask Beryl.'

'We found a body there. Might have heard about it on wireless.' Harry Noyes moved his head in such a way that it was neither a nod nor a shake. 'Not drowned though. Sandblasted to death.'

Harry remembered National Service. The noise, sparks and smell as sandblasters cleaned the corroded hulls of submarines in Rosythe Naval Dockyard. He felt ill. 'You think –'

'Come on, Mr Noyes. Charlie put that bloke's head through a breadslicer.'

'Never proved. Didn't even come to court.' This time

Charlie had gone too far. Hands perhaps, but not a head. Murder investigations stop everything. It had bankrupted their business.

Singleterry raised a finger and thumb. 'That makes it two. Take your pick.'

'Two what?'

'Murders, Mr Noyes. Feel free to choose. We don't mind charging you two with both, if you like. Two for the price of one. This week's special offer.'

A pair of lads on mountain bikes freewheeled down the hill. Harold Noyes closed his eyes and waited.

'We thought you might be able to indicate to us just who did commit them. It would not be grassing. For starters we wouldn't pay you, and you've already done your time. Does your Mrs Noyes know about the breadslicer? Does Charlie's Anna – Mrs Grice?'

Singleterry had him trapped. This time against his family. He had nothing left to hide from the police, but everything from them. He now wished he had let his brother breadslice Jack Singleterry. Too late now: his brother could never be left alone again.

'I'm getting cold,' Singleterry said. 'Very cold. Much as I love gardening, I hate being cold. Come on, let's have some names, Harry.'

'There are no names, Mr Singleterry.'

'How about Michael?'

'Out in Gambia. He's a partner in timeshare company.' That much Harry did know. No one was sure of its legitimacy, possibly not even Michael. He had sided with his mother after she divorced Charlie.

'And Patrick?'

'Gartree, for forged licence stamps.'

'Of course, I was forgetting.'

'You put him there, inspector.'

'Superintendent, please,' corrected Singleterry.

'I was forgetting,' replied Harry.

'You cheeky fucking bastard. You want this spade up your nose?'

The three men turned at the sound of a shed door opening. Charlie Noyes had finally managed to find a way to undo its latch. He couldn't quite remember the two strangers talking to his Harry. He wanted to tell Harry something. Something important, but the latch was so hard to open he had forgotten it. Perhaps they had come about the allotment: Harry was never very good at gardening. Each step Charlie took seemed to make them grow bigger, older. Had they come about the payments? He would have to remind Harry, put him straight. Where was he? He couldn't remember who any of these three men were. Suddenly there was too much to think about. There was a funny smell. Charlie Noyes turned to go back into the shed.

'Charlie!'

Charlie was confused. One of the three men sounded just like his brother. 'That you, Harry?'

'Course. Who did you think it were?'

'I don't know.'

'Let's go home, Charlie. It's getting late.'

'No. You said you'd finish veg patch and have you buggery.'

'We'll come back tomorrow.'

'You've paid bill?' demanded Charlie.

'Bill who? For what?'

'Bill at council. I told you, Harry. Pay bill for allotment.'

'Charlie, it's paid. You were there when I did it.'

'I was?'

'Charlie. Listen –'

'Who are these two men?'

'No one, Charlie. No one you'd know.'

'They're from council. Tell them you've paid bill. He's paid bill.'

'Listen. They've come to see me, haven't you, lads? That's all, nothing important. Come here, Charlie, and let's do your coat up. Anna'll have us supper ready, don't want it cold.'

The hands that had thrust a man's head screaming through a breadslicer struggled to fasten up his own coat. Trouser flies were left undone and the fresh air caught the smell of stale piss-soiled fabric. Alzheimer's, his brother explained as he pulled off his gardening gloves.

'Tell them we're not growing asparagus. Tell them we're not growing asparagus. Tell them!'

Jack Singleterry looked Charles Noyes straight in the eye as his brother worked up the buttons of his coat. Charles Noyes put his hands on Harold's shoulders and looked straight back. It all came together.

'I know you. I know you. You killed Freddie. You fucking killed Freddie, you fucking –'

'No, Charlie, no!' Harry held his wrists tight as he struggled to break free. 'Don't fight, don't fight.' They fell onto the half-dug vegetable patch. Charlie still tried to break away, Harry still tried to explain the past between breaths. 'You'll hurt yourself. Please Charlie, it were accident. Freddie died in an accident. We've told you before, we've been through this. Freddie died in accident.'

'An accident,' repeated DCI Naylor, ready to help Harry lift Charlie from the weeds and upturned earth.

'That's right, Charlie,' his brother soothed. 'A long time ago. Freddie died in accident.'

'Yes. Yes. No. Yes. A bad accident. Yes. Car crash.' Each word forced a tear to drop down Charlie's cheeks onto Harry's white curls while he bent down to do up the final button.

Naylor pulled at Singleterry's sleeve. It had been an accident. A bad accident.

Freddie had wanted to outdo his two elder brothers. He

robbed banks when everyone else believed banks were too crazy to rob. Too many alarms and security screens. His final robbery went well enough except an identical Cortina came and parked behind the getaway car. Freddie made a mistake anyone might make in a blinding hurry. By the time the poor driver was left shaking at the memory of a gun barrel in her face, the police had cordoned off Suffolk Park. Instead of reversing, Freddie drove straight through the third roadblock he met. Fearing for their lives, three authorized firearms officers fired at the Cortina. None of the fifteen bullets discharged hit Freddie. One shattered the windscreen, another punctured the nearside front tyre. The Cortina hit a garden wall at fifty-eight miles an hour. Frederick Noyes was not wearing a seat belt.

Naylor let Singleterry squeeze through the broken gate first. Things seemed to be going a bit better between them. Perhaps they could stop for a drink together. He noticed the faded council regulations. Under the grey polythene someone had underlined with a ruler and pale red ballpoint: '7.6 iii. Growing of Asparagus is strictly prohibited under all circumstances.'

Singleterry took a cigarette from Naylor but declined to light it. 'You didn't say much.'

'Didn't I?' Naylor didn't think he was meant to.

'You better not be feeling ill again.'

'No, I'm fine, Jack – superintendent. It's as though we've just walked over somebody's grave.' DS Naylor had been one of the three authorized firearms officers at the roadblock. DC Singleterry was absent, preparing to retake his sergeant's exam. 'It's sad about Charlie.'

'Sad? He sticks another bloke's head through a breadslicer and now he can't hold his own dick straight. Don't give me sad, I call that funny.' Neither of them laughed. 'Freddie, Frederick Noyes. What were name of his bastard driver? Blank Frank Miller. We'll see him next.'

*

Harry cleaned the spade and fork to stack them neatly back in the shed between some raspberry canes and a worn nitrate bag before padlocking its door. He did it exactly how his brother would have done.

'You've forgotten my flies,' said his brother. 'That's what I was meant to tell you. They're all bastards. I couldn't get latch up in time. Sorry.'

Underneath the coat Harry placed his brother's penis back inside his underpants. His trousers were wet through. The two brothers held each other in the deserted overgrown allotments. It seemed to Harry that the disease inside Charlie's head was eating his brother's personality away before his eyes. He heard the hills being sandblasted in Rosythe.

Halfway down Carrdyke Lane a two-year-old Rover saloon pulled up below the street lights in the murk before dawn. DC Wilet read its number plate: Customs and Excise were back on duty to relieve her. Double shifts were a killer, they pushed the Dark Peak into another world. She packed her belongings into her backpack, checking its side pockets for a key to unchain her mountain bike. They switched shifts quicker than it took her to fit lights onto her bike and ride away. There was nothing to report but the onset of more rain. Her partner would have gone to work by the time she got back home to bed.

A small ordinary van passed by as she turned left into Ingot Street. Tyres and wheels flexed over the potholes and iron inspection covers. She heard a brief gurgling noise. Probably just the drains, she thought.

Seven

Rain came to cover the city with a skin it didn't want. The railway station flooded several times and parks had become bogs. The streets threatened to turn into the rivers that had disappeared underneath the city.

It didn't stop the investigation. They sifted through and eliminated all the missing person reports in South Yorkshire. Singleterry had personally ordered them not to take a step beyond this boundary. John Tilt seethed. It was going to be a Sheffield murder regardless of the truth. Not that they had made any progress outside the police station either.

More than a month's round-the-clock observation of Carrdyke Lane had brought them nothing except a wet, lost but appreciative drunk. He'd thanked uniform when they moved him on. Neither the police nor Customs and Excise had noticed how the Mark of Zorro, Sheffield's notorious graffiti artist, had managed to spraycan his work onto the damp foundry walls, right beneath their very noses. 'Eat your hearts out' it read, in a lurid mixture of suggestive buttocks and Valentine hearts. Everyone had assumed it was there already before their shift. No one else stopped to pull up outside the empty building.

Towards dusk each Saturday a small ordinary van drove past the empty building without stopping. They made a note of its registration, just in case, but the van never stopped. It was amongst thousands of vehicles which regularly used Carrdyke Lane as a shortcut across the city, like the patrol car in the snow. Its registration plate was clean; its driver remained too scared to get out.

John Tilt walked their dog past the local vicarage. Empty too, up for sale. The diocesan solicitor had just informed the church wardens that their recently retired vicar had helped himself to the maintenance funds over the last twelve years. Ecumenical pensions being what they were, the incumbent had been tempted. Upon retirement he had to move out, of course, become homeless. The church was strapped for cash too: they wanted rid of this living.

Tilt examined the vicarage window frames: paint peeling off like dead skin, the wood itself soft, ready to mulch when pressed. Rotten to the core, like the police force, perhaps the church he had worked for. And within this moment he realized the fabric of his faith, so readily taken for granted, lay in disrepair, waiting to fall apart, collapse completely. Be washed away into nothing. He did not know how to repair the damage. He felt himself being pulled at the leash but did not want to go home either.

Staring down at his bare desk Detective Chief Inspector Naylor couldn't remember why he had joined the police. Jack Singleterry was right. It had seemed a simpler job when they had started; you just went out there and felt collars. Today they existed in a world of targets, outputs and deliverables: terms without meaning, words you could not interrogate, convict and lock up. He was getting old; he couldn't imagine what else to do.

Perhaps things should've gone a bit quicker. They'd have to get a result soon; their section couldn't carry the cost of the Reddlewood investigation into next year's budget. He started to go over the figures again, trying to make them add up. The investigation of costs had long since taken over the investigation of crime. Money hadn't been a problem in the old days. Nothing gave him gut-ache then. Bill Naylor unlocked the drawer holding the record cards he had borrowed from records without asking. Nowt. Charlie Noyes' kids weren't involved; Blank Frank Miller had disappeared. The cards didn't add up to the back end of a puppet theatre flat, never mind the exact découpage miniature of events that he liked to take with him to court. The usual shortcuts led nowhere.

Milk of magnesia tablets seemed to make matters worse. He'd run out again this morning. A spear of pain ran from his sphincter to just below his heart. Another thing for Mrs Eccles's shopping list.

No wonder they got nowhere fast. They had no plans to match their lack of resources. They weren't even a team. Just isolated people, scattered across a city. Each alone. Bill Naylor felt as anonymous as the many thousand index cards left in records. Perhaps Creeping Jesus was right. Perhaps they'd best hand it over to the Serious Crime Squad in Leeds. Try saying that to Jack Singleterry. The phone rang before DCI Naylor could grab his coat and disappear for the day.

'Yes, Mr Plummer, he must've routed his calls through to me. Detective Superintendent Singleterry has been very busy. I appreciate Customs and Excise require a meeting. It would help if we collated our information first, wouldn't it? Of course, I will tell him.'

Naylor rang upstairs.

'Jack. It's this pilchard Plummer. Can we talk? I'll get them in.'

Singleterry joined him at the bar ordering a second pint. Retirement wasn't far off, but Jack Singleterry wasn't ready to retire. He needed the edge that criminal investigations gave him to express his emotions. Not that he had many to express, still less to share. He hated too much to share. He hated his wife as he hated all women as he hated all men, hated parents, children, families, each living creature except himself. Hatred had become his profession, and in three years' time he'd have to retire. He'd hate that too. He knew he needed the safety of the force to protect him from the hatred of others. He preferred to make enemies where most people chose to make friends. He knew that's why he had joined the force. It had helped him to learn how to express hatred and love its expression. That's what made him a good copper. The best.

His wife hid from his enormous animosity beneath the paper world which came through their letterbox. She administered the household accounts, abridged the TV guide for him and circled tentative choices in holiday brochures. She wished he would leave her; she was far too frightened to hate him back. Instead she grew smaller and smaller every time she saw him. Only the hurt when he hit her helped make her feel alive, more real: she'd wait for the next time. They had no friends or children.

Her husband read little and wrote less. Throughout his career his atrocious typing masked his atrocious spelling. By hook, but more by crook, he scrummaged through police exam papers, and ignored everything else that was written down or printed, including rules and procedures, or statements previously made by witnesses or suspects. Especially suspects. The more he hated, the more they were guilty. It was as simple as that. His colleagues let him get away with it. His superiors respected him for his results, if not how he gained them. You're mad, Bill Naylor had thought, returning with the first aid tin, Harry Noyes' face made a bloody pulp *after* he had confessed. You're stark raving bonkers.

Driving a Rover 2000 pursuit vehicle up and down the M1, Probationary Constable Naylor had wondered whether Probationary Constable Singleterry actually saw straight. Motorway patrol meant page after page of vehicle index numbers each shift. It was dull, but Jack never got one registration plate right. It had been bad enough having to carry him through written assignments; here it was virtually impossible to cover for him.

'You must have word-blindness or something,' PC Naylor had said.

'Fuck word-blindness,' came the reply. 'Only dozy plods become trainspotters. There is nothing wrong with my eyes.'

There wasn't, it went deeper. Symbols on a page made Jack Singleterry feel dizzy, sick. Print hurt his brain, which screamed at the sight of words pushed into his face by primary teachers' chalk. At primary school Singleterry, J. never learnt that he suffered from dyslexia. Blackboard dusters aimed at his ears bruised the hurt. He taught himself how to throw them back. Singleterry used people like Naylor because he hated paperwork about as much as he hated people. The higher his rank in the force the easier it became to bury his word-blindness. To torture where he had been hurt.

'Fuck Customs and Excise. The way you drink, Bill, probably pays for that pillock Pilchard's wages.'

By the end of the next round they had figured out how to keep Mr Plummer out of harm's way for at least a fortnight.

Hussein Yassire and John Tilt bumped into one another walking across the cathedral yard. Each of them carried identical shopping bags from Waterstone's in Orchard Square. A chill breeze cut round corners but now it only threatened to rain.

'Two friends, John, gave me the exact same book this Christmas. It takes me this long to decide which copy to keep.'

Tilt laughed. He liked Yassire's dry, gentle and self-deprecating sense of humour. It survived less and less at home or in church. It had never existed within the police force.

'Sorry about the chair,' he said.

Yassire pushed back his bifocals. Scene of crime had failed to match the flecks of paint in the body to the office chair that the victim was tied to in the empty building. Scene of crime had managed to throw the chair out by mistake. It was far too worn to keep in their office. The Reddlewood case remained stalled.

'Worse things happen at sea. What's in your bag, John?'

'Paul Klee prints – Jen's favourite. A sort of belated Valentine.'

Not exactly true. Not true at all, but Tilt pushed on with the lie. They'd had a really bad row, so bad they didn't want to talk about it. Shift patterns kicked it off, how he was never there. He said he did his best but she stormed into the sitting room and he followed, their children transfixed in the kitchen. She took a book from a shelf and tried to beat him about the head. He had taken the book from her, ripped it in two and stared at her with fists clenched to leave for work without a further word. It was an art book, and the Paul Klee looked the closest Waterstone's had in stock.

In the arts section upstairs a poster of *The Prophetic Visions of William Blake* had caught John Tilt's eye. Monsters, daemons, fiends and their demigods chased the possessed. They seemed to yell at him to come closer. They seemed to say people must be hurt. He bought the Klee and followed Hussein Yassire down the High Street.

They said goodbye as the pathologist walked up Fargate Hill. Tilt watched a gaggle of gangers start to dismantle the jib of a crane over the remains of the Hole in the Road. They had erected here a huge scrap steel sculpture that had been commissioned for the stillborn business airport. Appropriately enough it was called *Flight of the Phoenix* and it had been on Sheff FM's breakfast show. His wife said she'd take their children to see it this weekend. He'd be on an early. That's how their row had really started: she said he thought more of the police and the church than her and their family. It hardly mattered whether it was true, its utterance made them both suddenly hate each other. Come back with a divorce, she yelled after him through the slam of their front door.

Walking back to the police station, Tilt thought he saw the diocesan solicitor at a window overlooking the cathedral yard as the wind howled through the sculpture. Half reptile, half bird, *Flight of the Phoenix* ripped through his mind. His thoughts raced between the visions of Blake to a vision of a sandblasted body hanging from the crane.

DC Wilet took a sip from a vending machine plastic cup. Other than being warm it was undrinkable. Hospitals were too often like prisons: no one wanted to go there. DC Wilet waited for her superiors. The Lone Ranger and Tonto, as Ruth had repeated to her partner in bed. Bill Naylor notably shorter, a step behind Jack Singleterry – they were more like a pantomime horse. Her partner had laughed too, holding Ruth in her arms as the rain hammered against their bedroom window.

The detective constable stared at an ambulance splashing by. Its crew were off for their break: a respite from A & E at the City General. Tied to rows of seats, fixed and hardened by hope and worry, were knots of friends, relatives and the ill, waiting to be set free. Ruth Wilet did not need to hope or worry but felt guilty for waiting. She knew that ordinary people must feel much the same about police stations. No one wants to go there either.

Blank Frank Miller had turned up face down in Edden Park. A tip-off to Staninglowe nick. The patrol car found Blank Frank exactly where the caller had indicated, behind the parks depot off Rushmere Road. They called an ambulance immediately. His back was hacked to pieces. Damp scraps of skin and clothes waited like dead leaves for the wind to blow them away. On the grass underneath the body they found a number plate which said GRASS.

The patrol car officers placed it in an evidence bag, then went back to discussing the evening edition of the *Sheffield Star*. Its back page explained how the flotation of Sheffield Wednesday left the Blades as the last big league team not quoted on the stock market.

Ruth Wilet watched an unmarked Vectra park in a bay designated 'Ambulance Only'. The Lone Ranger and Tonto got out to swear at the rain. She realized they always had to have something to swear at. Their hatred of others defined who they were.

'He's in casualty, sir,' she explained to the detective superintendent at the front end of the pantomime horse. Its back end tried to half hide behind its front end.

'I know that, you idiot. What's to stop us seeing him?'

'Nothing, sir. I've spoken to the charge nurse. He said Mr Miller's lost well over a litre of blood and the wounds to his back will require extensive stitching and skin grafts. His left lung's punctured and he's on oxygen. They intend to operate just as soon as they can get his condition stable. If he regains consciousness they'll knock him out again with the anaesthetic. I'll tell them you're here, sir, but the charge nurse has asked if we could contact his closest relatives. I've let uniform take care of that. He also wondered whether we knew Mr Miller's occupation. His injuries appear to have been sustained by machinery. Sir?'

The back end of the pantomime horse suddenly started to laugh uncontrollably. The front end turned angrily as the back end flicked a tear or two away from his eyes. 'It's obvious, Jack,' said Bill Naylor. 'The personalized number plate. Whoever Blank Frank grassed up must've found out and did him with a Flymo.'

Jack Singleterry croaked a laugh too. 'Poor Blank. He's like this girlie here – he'll find it hard to see the funny side of things.'

DC Wilet smiled. Over the shoulders of her superiors she watched the hospital car-park staff clamp their unmarked Vectra.

Eight

Somewhere inside the City General Frank Miller opted to regain consciousness. Sooner or later he'd have to. He didn't want to see his family suffer too much. Flat out and face down he could do without their sympathy, or anger. The next time a nurse brushed past he'd pinch her backside. He wouldn't be able to do much else for a while.

The nurse pinched his backside back. 'There's two coppers outside. Shall I tell them you're here?'

Frank Miller tried to piece together what had happened, but it made too much sense to take in. He allowed the pain control to take him back into unconsciousness.

Singleterry and Naylor caught up with the trolley leaving recovery.

'Hello, Blank,' Singleterry remarked, hanging his hat from the glucose drip. 'Don't bother to get up.'

Behind worn-out curtains inside a converted storeroom at the far end of Elliot Ward two nurses lifted Frank Miller onto a bed. Their patient demanded a solicitor.

'I don't think you do,' Singleterry shouted back through the curtains, 'unless you want to be charged with armed robbery.'

'Armed robbery?'

'Suffolk Park Estate. Eighty-one. With Freddie Noyes.' For regular customers like Blank Frank Miller, Singleterry always held a good solid case or two back in reserve. It kept them sweet. Fitting them up with makeweights in between simply doubled the results.

The nurse gave Singleterry his hat back from the trolley. 'Visiting hours are between two and eight.'

'Right. Who did this?'

'Who did what?' Frank Miller asked. 'I thought you knew.'

'Visiting hours are between two and eight.'

'That's all right, luv. We'll've done while then.'

'Well, we shan't,' replied the nurse. Uniform coppers were all right – she used to be one. Detectives remained nasty arrogant bastards. They didn't care about the law, still less other coppers.

'Come on, Frankie. For the record.'

'Sorry, Inspector Naylor, let me guess.' They ignored the nurse and let Frank play for time. 'You want me to tell you who cut me up, so they can find out and do me all over again.'

'"It's a lot less bovver with a hover," Frank,' quipped Singleterry. 'You should know.'

Frank Miller felt a catheter tube brush across the back of his thigh as its bag filled remorselessly. Never mind catching the bastards who did this, what he didn't understand was how the police didn't know who he'd grassed up. He remembered becoming a bundle in the back of a van. The metal floor covered in grass cuttings, the sweet smell of two-stroke mower oil and cigarettes. The law had failed him.

Bill Naylor tried again. 'Frank, none of us really want to return to Suffolk Park unless we have to. These people are dangerous.'

'You think I don't appreciate that already?'

'No, really dangerous, Frank. You could've finished up in the mortuary. They sandblasted their last victim to death. We still don't know who he is.'

'Castrated the poor sod,' explained Singleterry. 'Then blew his brains out through his eyes. Think yourself lucky, you've got away lightly with a little edge trimming. It's a lot less bovver with a copper.'

Franklin Miller closed his eyes and heard a starter cord buzz a two-stroke engine into life. Who else had the Stacy-Fisher consortium decided to discipline? No one he knew. This ought to mean he was still safe, relatively speaking. No one else was out to nail him – except the law. They were playing silly buggers, lucky-dipping for extra evidence. He wouldn't put anything past Singleterry and Naylor. Someone being sandblasted to death? Likely story.

The mower blades tore into his flesh. Sweat started to etch pain back into his wounds through the morphine drip. He metered it up to the maximum dosage. Everyone despises grasses. Especially themselves, for they know they've lost the trust of others. In return they can trust no one. It became too much: Blank Frankie Miller stopped trying to think straight, or crooked, and just talked.

The nurse's gentle cleansing of his wounds woke Frank up. 'What did I tell them?' he said to himself.

'Tell who?' she replied, although she had guessed he meant the two plainclothes.

'I can't remember. I can't remember. I can't remember anything after they Flymoed me.'

Her gloved fingers tried to slide the pain away from his body now the police had gone.

Singleterry strode ahead so fast that Naylor rushed to regain his breath while the lift doors opened.

'You're in the right place for a coronary. How did you pass the physical this year, Billy Boy?'

'Can't remember. Just did, I suppose.'

'Well, you better have remembered to have written down what Blank Frank told us, or you're fucked.'

They walked back down Cocker Wing to Leppard car park. It made sense. These days Frank Miller fenced more than he drove for other villains. All fences possess a tendency to grass in order to double returns: an occupational hazard well known to both sides of the law. Even so, most fences caught shopping their customers get away with a heavyweight kicking, common assault at worst. Fences are hard to come by and the kickers know that the fence, or the police for that matter, will hardly hurry to press charges. Grievous bodily harm inflicted at the sharp end of a Flymo indicated corporate action, not just a verbal warning to an awkward employee. Whoever Stacy-Fisher were, they weren't local. The four sets of boots who left the body seven weeks ago inside the empty building could be theirs. This time they had decided to include the law on their message's mailing list. They must have felt safe enough to do so. Best bring in this Mr Clemp from Barnsley that Blank Frank kept mentioning. They didn't need Serious Crime Squad pedal-to-metal down the outside lane from Leeds to steal their result. They were getting somewhere at last.

Jack Singleterry stared at the shiny yellow wheel-clamp, Bill Naylor at the notice stuck to their windscreen. Both had been affixed by Safe-Park PLC.

'Would you fucking believe it?' began Singleterry. 'Get taxi, Bill. Leave this to uniform.'

DCI Naylor checked his wallet for the fare. He knew he would have to fork out and claim it back. Singleterry had told him to forget all about pay and display when they arrived. There seemed to be a couple more ten pound notes than normal. He couldn't remember whether he had left Mrs Eccles her thirty pounds beside the kitchen sink with the weekly shopping list and washing-up. He couldn't really remember the weekend either. He'd woken up with really bad gut-ache. Mondays were getting worse.

CLEMP, *Colin Michael*. White; male; 38 years old; divorced; three children. Record: Six months inside Doncaster for assaulting a constable, 1984; two summonses for failure to pay maintenance; two for driving without tax and insurance, and failure to pay the fine; twelve counts drunk and disorderly.

Someone had scrawled 'NFB' across the top of his record card: Normal for Barnsley. Not a real villain, more a violent drunk.

Singleterry glanced at Naylor. Why should they know him? But now they did, they weren't about to take chances. Not with villains who had left Blank Frank Miller for dead.

'You'd better fetch me armoury chits to sign, Bill. Think Wilet's up to it? Girlies with guns.'

'What? Yes, sorry.' It was all happening a little too quickly. Bill Naylor wanted to go back to the pile of record cards locked away in his desk. Sheffield ended this side of the Tinsley Viaduct that carried the M1 in from Leeds. Colin Michael Clemp lay on the other side. Naylor couldn't remember the last time he had left Sheffield. He couldn't think of a reason to.

Detective Superintendent Singleterry countersigned the weapon release forms in triplicate. 'Don't shoot each other,' he said without a smile. 'You'd probably miss.'

'It's Jack's sense of humour,' Naylor explained, trying to keep up with Wilet going downstairs. 'NFS. Normal for Superintendents.' He sent her to fetch another car while he caught his breath waiting for the armoury duty officer to check the paperwork. Nerves. Firearms made everyone breathless, better to admit it than to deny or pretend otherwise.

'Both AFOs, currently validated. Release forms, each signed and countersigned. What would you prefer, sir?

Pistol or revolver. The superintendent has only put "Handgun".'

As usual he had left Naylor to fill in the rest. 'Does it matter, sergeant? As long as it works.'

'You'll need bullets then.'

Ruth Wilet returned to two Browning automatics with cartridges and shoulder holsters laid out precisely along the long counter like a couple of cordless electric drills in a tool-hire shop. Her training course kicked in and she viewed the weapons with clinical detachment. She had applied for the firearms course because she was scared, too scared to rely on other coppers with guns – and got top marks in her group. This was her first time out live.

'If you could check and load your weapons, please, then I shall authorize their release.' She and the sergeant exchanged looks. The DCI wasn't their idea of a marksman.

There wasn't exactly a problem with the cars: it was just that there weren't any. The reserve had gone to the City General to unclamp the one that Singleterry and Naylor had left there. 'Sir, there is a Transit fourteen-seater.'

Bill Naylor stopped loosening a shoulder holster strap to give DC Wilet a look which said Sheffield detective chief inspectors do not drive around in the station rowdybus. Not even if they are half-cut most of the time. It was against procedure but common practice in City Division to use personal vehicles on duty.

'We'll take mine, constable – no, we can't. It's at Dutton-Forshaw. Bit of a dent which needs fixing.' An ugly weal down the offside rear wing, reversing out of the senior officers' car park, the paint still left on the corner post. Naylor was still struggling with the shoulder strap.

'I think you'll find that buckle fits the other way round, sir.'

'You cycle to work, DC Wilet. That mountain bike thing.'

'Not today.' Ruth Wilet didn't know why she said it, but

as soon as she did, she wished she hadn't. It was her partner's car parked in the compound.

'Good. Yours it is then. No objections.'

Wilet shrugged her shoulders. It didn't matter what she said, the police force did what they liked. In silence the two detectives pulled their coats back on, over their guns.

It was just one of a hundred settlements between Worksop and Wakefield. Clots of terraces bled into small streets of shops. A school or a surgery perhaps, closed down against a dead space where the winding head had been. A bruised landscape each side of the M1. From the air their remains created regular, nearly archaeological patterns that followed rocks thousands of feet and millions of years below the surface. Pit villages once, now 'Coalfield Communities'. A name government in London had rubber-stamped across a map to solve a problem of their own doing. A map of nameless dots. Dots that flooded pits for ever. It wasn't Sheffield, it was nowhere. Dots and people no one else ever cared about.

Here it was different. Opencasting had ripped out the fields the dead mines had tunnelled under.

Bill Naylor stared down at it all, and spoke out aloud to no one in particular. 'My dad were a Bevin Boy – you wouldn't know what I'm talking about. He went down pit at fourteen, during war. All his life he worked down pit. Pneumoconiosis got him before he were forty.' Naylor remembered the cough that had racked both their bodies as he sat perched on his father's bony shoulders. 'I came home from school each day to hear him breathe to death. His lungs rattled like rain against windows on a windy night. Slowly filling up like a pit itself. "Don't work in pit," he said. "Join army or police. Don't work too hard to kill yoursel'." One night the rain stopped and that were it.' Tears welled in his eyes. 'Friday Street, wherever that is.'

They very nearly missed it as they went into the village. Wilet parked opposite the house, and they waited two or three minutes to prepare themselves and check for movement behind curtains. With firearms it was best never to rush.

Naylor rapped the knocker twice, while Wilet stood to the left of the frosted glass door, ready to draw her weapon, as per procedure. A large dog barked and a gruff voice yelled even louder to tell the dog to shut it. Eventually the hands of a fat shadow shot back two bolts, a mortise and a Yale, all blurred through the glass. This had been replaced recently, to go with the work-boot indentations around the locks. Remnants of a domestic: normal for Friday Street. The door opened as far as its chain would allow. A woman shouted through the six-inch gap.

'He's not here.'

'Who?'

'Him. What's it to you?'

'We're police,' stated Naylor, showing his warrant card.

'Good, and about time too. He's not here.'

'Can we come in, Mrs Clemp?'

'Not unless you want our Colin's dog on you. Right mad, he is.'

'Can you tell us where he is then, please, madam?'

'Front room, chewing carpet.'

'Your son, Mrs Clemp. Not his dog.'

'Why didn't you say?' Mrs Clemp pulled the door hard against the chain to squash her head into the gap. 'Airport Van Hire. Back up road, turn left, down hill and second on right past Wagstaffe's. Can't miss it.'

'Thank you.'

'Tell him you're from Child Support Agency. That'll really put shit up the selfish bastard.'

Wagstaffe's Non-Ferrous Scrap had closed down too.

Tall corrugated-iron gates chained to each other, waiting to fall. Naylor looked lost to Ruth Wilet as they followed the narrow peninsular of derelict land that threaded through the blackness of empty opencast workings. They'd planned to reclaim them for the City Airport but the consortium had gone bust, leaving an enormous hole across the landscape.

Mrs Clemp was right, you couldn't miss Airport Van Hire. A caravan sat on bricks next to a derelict filling station, the only building still standing. Ruth Wilet drove through the open gate in the shiny new security fencing.

Colin Clemp lifted his eyes from a dead edition of the *Sunday Sport*, his ears tracking a car's careful deceleration. He had started as a one-man decorating and removal company – 'Clemp & Co' daubed down each side of a clapped out Transit, although he was never quite sure what the '& Co' stood for. Hundreds of ex-miners had latched onto the idea already, to struggle against the same men they had shared a lift-cage, coalface and pithead baths with. Competition was hard. Standards and prices, never high in the first place, plummeted. Clemp & Co found themselves out of business almost before they started.

One evening in the Old Welfare a stranger asked him to do some work. Black people almost never came to the Welfare. The place had fallen silent as he walked to the bar. Clemp was impressed: that took some bottle. He said ta to a pint and they started talking. Colin wanted to be in with this, it was big time. Alone under the street lights and their cracked shadows Clemp said he'd think about it. 'Don't think too long,' said the black man. 'I hate this place.' Clemp nodded his head; it was his way out.

He'd never been abroad before. Ibiza twice, for honeymoons, but that didn't count. Cash in hand, he nurtured the Transit's clatter back through Dover, full of tobacco, beer and spirits, then up the motorway to an abandoned petrol station. It was the simplest three hundred pounds he had ever earned and it was perfectly legit. 'How about petrol money?' he asked, and they gave him that too.

They trusted him. That was all he needed to know. In the space of a year they helped him set up a small business at the abandoned petrol station. Airport Van Hire was his idea. 'Call it what you like,' they said. 'Just do as we say.' He did. More recently, every other trip he'd bring back a passenger who'd leave with an overnight bag almost as soon as they passed through customs. 'If anyone should ask, we're mates. If anyone should.'

Colin Clemp kept the Transit but bought a 1982 Audi Quattro Coupé, dropped its suspension, tinted its windows and sprayed it starburst metallic purple. You are what you drive, they told him in the Welfare. With all the spare cash he could make his maintenance payments too, but he let Psycho chew up the letters. Instead he started to put aside some of the boxes from the Transit, just one or two from each trip. They'd never notice, they trusted him. The boxes piled up, filled the inspection pits in the abandoned garage. He'd need to shift some of them, move them on. Give this Frank Miller another ring.

He heard the car pull into the yard. Clemp hurried to the window and hurried back again. He had never seen these two before. Newish car, man and a woman fairly well dressed in smartish suits, probably from the Child Support Agency. He wasn't going to wait to find out. He had told his mum not to say where he was, the cow.

DC Wilet reacted first. 'Stop,' she shouted. 'Police, Stop!'

Clemp didn't bother to stop. Wilet drew her weapon. Behind the wheel of the Quattro he rushed to start the engine.

'Shut the gates,' yelled Naylor. 'Shut the fucking gates on the bastard.'

They heard the starter motor whine for about five to ten seconds, then the turbo howl into life. As Wilet was steadying herself to fire first at the tyres then at the dark tinted windows, the car exploded into a tower of flame and hurled their suspect through its windscreen.

Naylor and Wilet were starting to reholster their firearms and rush to their suspect's aid when three large dark metallic cars screamed up to the garage gates.

'STOP!' a loudhailer called. 'ARMED POLICE. STOP! DO EXACTLY AS YOU ARE TOLD AND NO ONE WILL BE HARMED.' At least three semi-automatic carbines were aimed directly at them.

Inside his own head Bill Naylor jumped back twenty years and saw Freddie Noyes driving a dark blue 1.6XL Cortina straight towards him.

'RAISE YOUR HANDS SLOWLY AND AS FAR AS THEY WILL GO. NOW KNEEL DOWN. YOU – DROP THE GUN.'

'I think I've just shit myself,' Naylor whispered to himself.

Wilet said nothing. She had already turned, assessed, aimed and was about to fire at the hearts of the first three targets. Then she noticed the small blue 'Police' decals on their bullet-proof jackets. She felt her pee soak through her knickers to dampen her trousers and thighs. She was too angry to cry. She dropped the gun.

Between them and the gates Colin Clemp regained consciousness and started to scream more loudly than the roar of his blazing car. Desperation had saved his life. A seat belt would have incinerated him.

'For Christ's sake,' Naylor shouted, 'we're fucking police too. Call an ambulance.'

'DO AS I SAY. LIE FACE DOWN WITH YOUR LEGS AND ARMS AS FAR APART AS THEY WILL GO. NOW!'

An ambulance siren echoed across the black empty space, reaching towards the narrow peninsular to mingle with the smell of burnt car and its burnt owner's screams. Below the noise Wilet and Naylor listened to a fraught tumble of boots until a group of shadows passed over them. Gloves roughly ran down their bodies to remove their wallets and authorized firearms.

Ruth Wilet closed her eyes and waited. She saw the corpse from blasting bay six chase her down endless diagonals of lighter-coloured tiles.

'Get up.'

They got up. Two of the three marksmen tried to dowse the embers of the burnt-out Quattro. The third helped the paramedics with Colin Clemp. The two Sheffield City detectives looked up to three tall figures dressed in identically cut immaculate coal-black suits which matched their dark glasses and large dark cars. The tallest nodded to her colleagues, who handed back their wallets but not their firearms.

'Detective Chief Superintendent Birtels, Serious Crime Squad, Leeds.' For the sake of completeness she showed them a warrant card to match her West Yorkshire accent and her black IC3 identity. 'Before you attempt to explain how you came to be involved in our operation, perhaps you could shed some light on the whereabouts of a Ms Rachael Sissens?'

'Rach?' said Ruth Wilet. 'Rachael? What's she – is she all right? She's my girlfriend, ma'am. Partner. That's her car.'

'Romeo Eight Four Seven, November Foxtrot Bravo. Registered keeper a Ms Rachael Sissens, 12 Halliwell Gardens, Bexleyheath, Kent. We have reason to believe it was stolen.'

'Can I try to explain?' interjected DCI Naylor. 'No other vehicles were available. It seemed –' He stopped. It made no sense to reason with a world gone mad. He should have taken the Transit. Stopped Jack Singleterry flouting rules everywhere he went, even in the hospital car park. Forced him to talk to the Leeds Serious Crime Squad in the first place. Not dented his own car. Easier said than done.

Anger displaced shock; Ruth Wilet had realized how it had all happened. The heads of City Section, Sheffield and the Serious Crime Squad, Leeds had not bothered to tell each other that they were investigating the same case. She wanted to throw her warrant card down the deepest hole in the world. They could shove it.

'You were concealed in Wagstaffe's yard, ma'am.'

'Yes – who told you, detective constable?'

'No one. We're detectives. It escapes me how someone managed to plant a bomb under Mr Clemp's car when you so clearly had Airport Van Hire under close surveillance.'

DCS Birtels blushed a dark crimson. It was bad enough local coppers messing everything up. This was too much.

A small man in an old-fashioned overcoat and trilby walked towards them from the old garage buildings. 'Best to search those inspection pits.' He looked over his rimless spectacles at DCI Naylor. 'Is this the major turf war your Superintendent Singleterry seems so reluctant to tell me about?' The man stretched out a hand. His hat was just like Jack's. 'Forgive me, Inspector Naylor. Mr Plummer, Customs and Excise. Nice to put a face to a name.'

Nine

It was Tilt's day off. Instead of spending it at home he sat alone in the empty vicarage. He had promised the diocesan solicitors to go through all the old bills and letters he could find. They lay piled up on the dining-room table as he tried to make some sense or order out of them. It was a mess, and he didn't know why he had volunteered to sort it out.

There were reasons: he was a church warden, he had the skills of a trained detective, it was the right thing to do. But these were just reasons, not the truth. The truth was he didn't know, or wasn't prepared to admit it. Something he could complete, finish, solve: unlike the Reddlewood murder. Something to take him out of the house. His wife took the book of Paul Klee prints from him without a word: they had not begun to talk about their row last week. In other words, one more pile of unfinished business to avoid. The truth was that having discovered the foundations of his faith and marriage were about as rotten as the vicarage window frames, John Tilt was too frightened of losing both to bear their close examination. He was a cautious man.

The sound of Calendar News drifted in from the next room. It made Tilt irate. He had specifically told their son to switch the TV off before leaving to go home. Nobody listened to him. Their son, daughters, Naylor, Singleterry . . .

Singleterry. His voice forced John Tilt to drop dead papers and rush to look at the TV screen in the lounge. A news conference inside City Division Headquarters. Camera flashes pulsed into the eyes of Detective Chief Superintendent Birtels and Detective Superintendent Singleterry, who sat behind their printed name labels with an empty chair between them. They shared a look that said it would remain empty for ever. They had nothing else to share, except how they had managed to screw up each other's operations completely. Singleterry resumed his inexpert reading of a prepared statement.

Tilt watched carefully as Jack Singleterry's index finger struggled to heave each word from the page and expel it through awkward lips. It merely made the Airport Van Hire fiasco all the more believable.

'May I assure everyone that this explosion is not the work of any known terrorist organization. As we speak, officers are apprehending those suspected of carrying out this heinous attack.'

Journalists paused, pens hovering above notebooks, to fathom the meaning of the phrase '*he in us*'. Singleterry was doing his level best to read the words that were there.

'I'd also like to stress that this operation is an excellent example of co-operation between the Serious Crime Squad, Customs and Excise and the City Division in the fight against drugs-related crime, particularly the organized trafficking of illegal substances, which, as we all know, is a nationwide problem that crosses city boundaries.'

Then Singleterry had to face their questions.

'How is the victim?'

'As well as could be expected.'

'Is he one of your suspects?'

'As of this moment I cannot comment,' admitted Singleterry.

The flash lights stopped. Reporters exchanged knowing

glances out of camera. In the vicarage Tilt switched off the TV. The law had made their usual Horlicks of it.

Neither Birtels nor Singleterry spoke a word until DC Kirk had ushered the last reporters from the room. In Leeds DCS Celene Birtels had heard all about Jack Singleterry; he had that sort of reputation throughout Yorkshire. She'd never wanted him anywhere near this operation. She had never told him a thing. They slowly turned to face each other.

Singleterry couldn't care less about his reputation or anything else. He told Kirk to find the detective chief superintendent a nice cup of tea. She wanted to take Singleterry into the station yard and beat the living daylights out of him. He knew that. That's why he asked Kirk to fetch her a nice cup of tea.

'I don't suppose you'd like to tell us about any more sandblasted bodies left lurking in empty buildings?' Birtels began. She had only just heard of the Reddlewood case.

'No, ma'am. You're right, I would not like to tell you. Care to explain why we were not kept informed of an operation where two of my officers were very nearly blown to pieces in pursuit of their duties?'

DCS Birtels did not reply. Jack Singleterry waited for her to button her coat. She didn't.

'Then to be held at gunpoint by the Serious Crime Squad? Ma'am.'

'Airport Van Hire lies outside Sheffield jurisdiction.'

'So does JFK. You didn't tell us about Frankie Miller being your snitch either.'

'Who did? Superintendent.'

'No one. Someone Flymoed Blank Frank for grassing them up. You didn't know, did you?'

Both officers stopped, stunned by the extent of their mutual ignorance. Entirely through deliberate concealment they had blocked each other out, kept themselves in the dark around the clock. An eclipse of such planetary blackness, yet until now it had seemed as ordinary to them as night following day. Nothing untowards – only that they had duped each other completely.

Singleterry was the first to react. 'Chief Superintendent Birtels. I find someone to blame, you stay out of Sheffield.'

'I don't give a monkey's. SCS is after Stacy-Fisher.'

'Stacy who?'

'Stacy-Fisher Property Management,' she explained patiently. 'Moss Side yardies. How are you going to keep them out?'

'We're not. You are, chief superintendent. The Serious Crime Squad's extensive network of informants and contacts will lift their dingly-dangly dreadlocks, pin back their ears and tell them it's six months' remand minimum for sandblasting some poor bastard to death.'

'You have no case.'

'You know that, I know that and for all I care they know that. CPS doesn't. You've not met our Detective Inspector Tilt. Nice chap. Christian. Devout, honest, God-fearing. A pillock – but in the witness box believed by every judge and jury in Christendom, silly sods. He'll get it to court, probably convicted. Stacy who? Ma'am.'

'You bastard. You get all the credit.'

'Of course. Who'll get the blame for not spotting the bomb which blew Colin Clemp into the City General? Right under the noses of the Serious Crime Squad. Were it to come to inquiry, ma'am, even the most senior officers might have to be called to book.'

Singleterry offered Birtels a cigarette after lighting up himself. They were both tall, sallow creatures. She looked him in the eye and refused.

'We're on same side, remember,' he remarked, blowing smoke through her hair.

'Except we hate each other. Let's be straight as well as rude, superintendent. Is it because I'm not a man or because I'm not white?'

'Neither, ma'am. Your being a black girlie doesn't mean I'm prejudiced,' he lied. 'I couldn't care less what you are. Black, Paki, queer, spaz, yid or lezzie makes no odds.' He threw the cigarette end at her feet. Hurt was a drug and he an addict. 'I'm not racist. I hate everybody.'

Birtels glared back. She failed to see a weakness.

'It's nothing personal, ma'am. Here's your nice cup of tea. Now fuck off back to Leeds.'

DCS Birtels took the cup from DC Kirk and threw it straight into Singleterry's face.

Ten

The walls of his office carried shelf after shelf of catalogued boxfiles. They surrounded the city coroner's desk. He was imprisoned by their discovery, and sentenced to their cause. His fingers touched the edges of the post-mortem report, as though physical contact with the printed page would lead him to witness the murder itself.

'entirely naked . . . the scalp and eyes had been pulverised and dispersed . . . castrated alive . . . it is difficult to comprehend the sensory and intellectual damage the individual endured . . . for upwards of two hours during the attack.'

His hands trembled. They wanted no more of it. They buried the report underneath the letter from Detective Inspector Tilt. Turning it over, the city coroner drafted a reply for typing, informing him of the date of the inquest and of his agreement that it be held in camera. He never touched a piece of paper more than once. It would not remain long within these walls.

The case had been buried. Quite neatly, just before the start of the next financial year, with zero budgetary implications. Singleterry and Naylor made sure of it. Customs and Excise, the Serious Crime Squad, the Moss

Side Stacy-Fisher consortium had served their purpose. City Section had survived. Their investigations were over, filed away. Dead paperwork.

They would never know the body's identity. The names or the number of murderers. They knew nothing. It did not matter. Never touch a body more than once. Murder silences itself.

John Tilt could not close the case inside his head. It remained open like the door to the toolshop office that led to the stairs and gantry to blasting bay six. It seemed like yesterday, only the snow had disappeared. British Summer Time had come and passed them by, but no one in their office had bothered to put the clocks forward. The case had been abandoned like its victim, its head pulverized into a broken clock face, smashed and stoved in. Time seemed to have closed down.

It hadn't stopped raining for weeks. It grew harder and harder, more insistent, as though each day's downpour was added to the next, until all that remained in the sky and the city was cold, hard rain. Inside their office they waited for the final rites. There was nothing else to do.

'Inspector Tilt. You need a change,' stated Bill Naylor.

Tilt nodded. It was unquestionably true. He was getting to look nearly as bad as Naylor.

'Records.' They both knew it was a shove sideways. 'Division are at us to update the Sex Offenders' Register.' They wanted him out of the way. 'This business with your church vicar.'

Word had got round. Been used. Tilt as a church warden, a position of some responsibility, might be implicated.

'Charges aren't to be pressed,' he protested.

'I know,' Naylor said. 'There might be an internal disciplinary.'

They both knew the threat was there. DCI Naylor had taken the next step, of bringing it out into the open. Tilt felt in his pocket for the letter from the city coroner's office confirming the date of the inquest.

Never touch a piece of paper more than once. The city coroner applied this rule to the inquest itself. It lasted three minutes. With murders the less mentioned before trial the better. Please make the necessary arrangements with the City Cemetery, the coroner instructed the recorder. DI Tilt was the only other person in a court of empty chairs.

Three minutes to ask about death. No time at all. It had taken over two hours to sandblast everything out of the victim. For some reason Tilt didn't want to leave the empty room. He was scared. Not by blasting bay six; of being a policeman.

The inquest was over but they could not bury the body. The city no longer buried nameless deaths: cremations were cheaper. The supervisor of the City Cemetery invoiced the city coroner for the costs of the cremation. The city coroner's office passed this on to the City Police. The secretary for the assistant chief constable passed it on to Detective Superintendent Singleterry, who left it for Detective Chief Inspector Naylor to pass on to Detective Inspector Tilt. It was records. The detective inspector read the letter back to the city coroner's office, and then to the City Cemetery. Each refused to pay. It was the responsibility of the family of the deceased: they really ought to have been billed by the finance department. Tilt phoned the finance department. Try the City Cemetery or the city coroner's office, they advised.

More through anger than argument, DI Tilt got through to the city treasurer.

'Inspector, there is a procedure for this sort of thing.'

'There may well be,' replied Tilt. 'It's called common sense.'

The city treasurer tried to overlook the paperwork hiding his desk. He had just returned from lunch to watch the rain pour down the gutters into the street below. This minor matter would not wash away and disappear. 'Send me the invoice and I'll see that it's paid.' He put the receiver down quickly. He'd been late for work this morning and had been pulled over for speeding.

Tilt decided to attend the funeral. Entering it into his diary, he doubted if he'd have chosen to go had life at home or work been a little easier, less stuck. Maybe out of plain Christian duty or a desire to see something completed, but probably not when all was said and done. Tilt was wrong. Although he scarcely realized it, he had become increasingly attracted to the murder ever since its discovery. He needed to understand cause as well as effect. Six blasting bays lay silent. Their enormous noise of aggregate, air and liquid still keen to flail bare flesh. Tongues of grit ready to split steeled lips. To wash all away. Beneath the dry cleaner's clear polythene cover his fingers felt the fabric of his darkest suit to double-check it had been cleaned and pressed.

Top deck bus windows peered over the City Cemetery walls as they crawled their way up Stillgate Hill. If anyone watched, they saw John Tilt walk slowly between the headstones, shoulders hunched like a fossil collector in search of an extinct yet undiscovered species, a missing link. He'd taken the last of his annual leave to attend the funeral. It seemed the right way to try and repair faith in his marriage, profession and God. He needed to move on. He adjusted the knot of his black tie. The idea that he was already trapped had yet to haunt him.

He stopped at the redbrick crematorium at the end of its gravel drive and stared at the building. Scarcely larger than a conservatory, vestigial oriel windows and architraves made it seem smaller and darker than it was. Although he worshipped a God who was eternal and all alive, John Tilt felt that death conspired to diminish the Church. He waited, feet apart, his fingers intertwined in front of his stomach, for others to arrive, just to one side of a pair of narrow plain oak doors. Suddenly he wished he had worn a hat. Not out of respect or custom; something to hold onto once inside. At least he had instructed the cemetery to order a Christian ceremony.

A tired grey hearse pulled itself through the cemetery gates. It seemed to change colour as it twisted through the graveyard, from the darkness of the headstones to the lesser grey of the scattered clouds above. A little way behind, a small off-white van followed. Probably maintenance, the detective inspector thought, glancing down at his watch. He could not decide if he was early or they late. Heavy tyres slowly crushed gravel into gravel. Their sound gradually climbed past the traffic crossing up and down Stillgate Hill. The rest of the world travelled away from here.

The small off-white van turned left at the entrance to the crematorium. The tired grey hearse stopped to reverse towards its doors. Four pallbearers, each wearing wire-framed dark smoked glasses and short greying ponytails, got out. They used to be a semi-professional heavy metal band. They slid the plain coffin onto their shoulders.

A young curate walked towards the narrow doors, head down, unaware of anyone watching, until he nearly bumped into the detective inspector. They knew each other. Not well: the curate was a diocesan stop-gap in Tilt's parish, for births, weddings and funerals, where lay priests could not officiate. They had hardly spoken.

Did Mr Tilt know the deceased? John Tilt did not know how to reply.

'No, not quite,' he eventually answered.

The curate shot across a sharp look. DI Tilt outlined his involvement, then offered to show his warrant card from a raincoat pocket. The curate waved it away. Had they found the murderer? No, just the body.

Sandblasted to death. Without that they wouldn't be here.

Tilt left it unsaid.

The pallbearers watched the curate fumble through a large bunch of scruffy old keys. One of them coughed, another scuffed the soles of his dark shoes against the gravel. They always take too much time; clerics never understand there are other funerals in other places to attend to. The dead don't stop dying just because you happen to bury a few of them. Finally the right key turned the right lock.

Light did not appear to enter or escape the crematorium. Colour disappeared. Cold, damp air leant against a giant heat. Enough to turn death into a handful of ash. Not enough to keep out the wind.

Tilt saw the young curate shiver. Before ascending a single-step pulpit, the curate asked him if he wanted to say a word. What sort of word? Who will miss the deceased? Who will mourn his passing? Who will help? It was not like pressing a suit. Tilt shook his head but stood close, nearest the window which appeared to give most light.

The pallbearers entered last, plain wooden coffin upon their shoulders, black-ribboned hats under their free arms, smoked glasses staring immutably forward. In their shadows, this odd eight-legged creature, half-beast, half-ourselves, searched for a break or passage within the service to disappear somewhere inside our thoughts – a moment for departure. The pallbearers rested the coffin upon cold rollers wearing through a threadbare carpeted belt. Almost without waiting for the curate's signal, a pair of bearers started solemnly to step backwards outside, to a simple chimney disguised as a Gothic spire. No spades, no lowering of wooden boxes into earth, no mud on shoes and trouser-legs; cremations were easier. Just turn up the gas and go. The curate gave them the signal.

A pair of feet passed the two pairs going out. The curate began the standard ceremony. He quickened his pace to try and overcome the absence of mourners. It failed. Words became harsh, metallic, to shatter against brick and stone; lips stumbled against the emptiness of air.

Tilt stared at the blank coffin as he prepared to pray. Machine-cut wood. Not planed or sanded, still less varnished; knots waiting to be filled. The grain uneven, coarse to touch. Grit and blood below the gantry as his hand raised the regulation incident sheet. Tilt failed to pray.

The remaining two pallbearers slowly pushed the box along the threadbare carpeted rollers through the shadow of curtains into the roar of eternal flame. Gone. The entire case, even the Polaroid photographs, seemed to burn away to nothing.

Suddenly Tilt felt a disappointment neighbouring on loss. He'd come no closer to solving the case, to knowing it was over. He had wanted to touch the body.

Outside, a haze of ash disappeared into a grey-blue sky. No scent or smell. No slightly charred aroma of abraded flesh as the air seemed to shiver with the far off noise of the city. Tilt remembered how the eyeless eyesockets had stared straight through him into blasting bay six. Its body had now gone, the enticement to return and stay close remained. A statue of evil carved from flesh. He should have touched it.

The young curate had to hurry. Christenings and funerals left him with a frantic urge to pee. Especially funerals. Dust to dust, ashes to ashes, his own body turned to water. Key in hand, he pulled the pair of doors to. Too quickly, and the oak jambs stuck together, twice. Tilt turned round as the cleric walked away from the sound of doors closing.

The stranger watched their white faces. He had slipped

past without their noticing. He hadn't meant to surprise them. He wasn't certain if he had intended to see them. He was not sure what to do. He turned to leave and stopped. He had lived here for too long and he did not know how to leave. The body had been burned, consumed completely, and he believed that this would free him, but the sky, the earth, the rivers and the seas, the entire earth he had known, had not changed a fraction. It was over and he was still trapped. If he stood still for long enough, he believed he might in the end disappear.

John Tilt stared at the tall black man without quite making eye-contact. Where had he come from? Why was he here? Well-dressed, expensively dressed – dark suit, white shirt, black tie and gloves – dressed for the part. He was holding a small wreath of rich tight flowers. His dark grey coat, thick, plain and heavy, seemed to fit him and the occasion perfectly. No thread out of place, the white and black hairs wrinkled at the temples like wire in a breeze. They matched tribal scars, narrow zig-zag rectangles on each cheek. They were about the same age, the other maybe a little heavier and younger than Tilt.

The stranger's eyes were still and glazed. Tilt decided to take a step closer to check for signs of alcohol, drugs. There were none. Instead he found himself staring into the emptiness of pain.

Without warning, the lips of the stranger started to move quickly. Far too quickly to compose serious speech; words which could be understood or followed. They were mumbles to themselves. Without a sound, without interruption. The sun snapped through the rain-grey sky, sharpening their faces. Tilt waited patiently, at first believing it might cease, make sense, merely an extended stammer into the wind. Seconds became minutes, the thuds and wails of the distant city starting to possess more reason. A mad man: the detective inspector had helped

101

section enough poorly medicated schizophrenics to recognize the symptoms – not just the silent mumblings and glassy stare, but the tic-like facial movements in a body too rigid to control itself. Then they ceased.

'I knew him,' the stranger suddenly announced in a slow rounded African voice. 'I thought you would bury him. What shall I do with this?' He held out the wreath.

Despair touched the tall stranger's voice. Tilt tried to understand.

'I did it,' the stranger whispered. 'I had to.'

The hearse left the cemetery to join the traffic on Stillgate Hill.

'Had to do what?' asked Tilt. He did not believe the African and the murder could be connected. He didn't want to consider it; he needed it to be all over. So did the African, which was why he had come. Tilt stared at the dark leather gloves grasping the wreath of dark crimson roses. He repeated his question. 'Why did you come here?'

'Today?'

The stranger did not know who Tilt was but it made no difference. He tried to say more but something held him back. Perhaps the closeness of death, that nothing he said or did could ever make a difference, not when it hardly had before. That's what drove him crazy – the something he was trying to say held him back from saying it. It double-bound his tongue against his palette. He tried to summon rain and darkness from the heavens, to hide himself inside the earth for ever. Instead he felt his lips start their mumbling. His eyes closed and he saw a Polaroid photograph take colour and shape. A still print of the murder. He realized Tilt would find it hard to accept the truth of blasting bay six.

'I killed him.' His eyes opened. They were like glass.

'I had to come here.' The glass shattered into tears. 'I had to make sure he was dead.'

Part Two

Eleven

Thirty-two years ago he had waited for a darkened oak door to open. It stretched far above his head, forcing him to feel smaller, as well as more isolated than the other boys. The busts of dead heroes: Julius Caesar, Shakespeare, Newton, Nelson, Wellington, Rhodes and Livingstone, together with the recent addition of Sir Winston Churchill, looked down on him from the entrance hall's cold panelled walls. The Cutlers' School knew who to respect. He had been summoned to senior school out of a history lesson. The pictures in its textbook, of William invading this strange land, the arrow in Harold's eye, stayed in his mind. His hands touched the cast-iron radiators. Frozen: the boilers were never lit before Christmas. They devoured heat to make a cold place colder, they seemed to devour any warmth or life left behind. The door opened. The child had already guessed why he had been called.

The Cutlers' forbade television; use of the wireless in the prep school house lay at their headmaster's discretion. Illegal transistor radios were punished by confiscation and the cane. The boy occasionally had a chance to look at the newspapers in the library: the odd column inch tucked away in the Colonial or African sections of the foreign news pages in *The Times* and the *Daily Telegraph*, deprecating the deaths of millions of his peoples between the Niger and Benue in Nigeria. Bullets aimed straight through their brains, rather than a single errant arrow in the eye. The English and French had sold them the bullets, trained them in their dispatch. They had kept quiet. Maintained a diplomatic silence, while, already decayed, the dead lay dumped in a mass grave that covered the land. Without salvage, even of their names.

The boy had turned each yellowing page of newsprint over and over. He read a second leader headed 'The political cancer of civil war' which disparaged the Commonwealth's efforts to negotiate with the White Rhodesia of a Mr Ian Smith. The English broadsheets trod the spent cartridge cases of the Biafran War into a past deeper than the Battle of Hastings. News travels fast, straight over his head and into history.

There were no pictures inside these newspapers. No clear-cut images of the horror and brutality, famine and disease that a twentieth-century African civil war brings, except inside the head of this eleven-year-old boy. They were the only things he had managed to take with him across Europe. The Red Cross had failed to deliver any letters from his family since last summer.

Harold Cedric St John Somerville stared across his desk at the small Nigerian boy. Somerville had managed to escape military service in two world wars. Apart from reading classics at Magdalen, he had spent his entire life from thirty-six months old inside English public schools, either being taught or teaching. It was home. It was safe. Especially as headmaster. He could scarcely pronounce Adtombwe's name, and he had no idea how to deal with the boy himself: the black face, the black hands, and the black knees protruding from his short trousers.

'Your shoelaces are tied incorrectly,' he began. The boy looked down. The approved means to fasten a bow remained a mystery. 'Don't worry about it now.'

Somerville always wore a sombre morning suit and wing

collar. He would feel naked in school without them. He stared back down to the letter from the Swiss bank of the boy's father: Schröedingers. A stout name for a foreign concern; it seemed worthy of his trust. After all, as Somerville had told himself earlier, the Swiss had also managed to avoid military service in two world wars, if not longer. He'd feel safe enough with Schröedingers who, in textbook English, explained the situation:

Dear Sir,

It is with regret that we must write to you upon behalf of the estate of our client, Romanus Adtombwe. We have received instructions from neither himself nor his agents in Kaduna for a continuous period of twelve calendar months. Prior this hiatus, our client had advised ourselves that, in view of the domestic situation current within his homeland, certain measures contingent upon absence of instruction, would come into effect.

His eldest son shall require a guardian until the age of majority (unless instructed otherwise by our client, Mr Adtombwe Senior). The Bank understands that The Cutlers' School acts *in loco parentis*. On the behalf of Mr Adtombwe Senior may the Bank respectfully request that The Cutlers' School consider this matter at its convenience.

Many thanks for your kind time and due attention.

Now Harold Cedric St John Somerville regretted his insistence on taking responsibility for the whole of this strange boy's school career from the start. It should have been a matter for Congreave, the head of the prep school. He had no idea how to explain this. He glanced at Congreave, who stood impassively just inside the door, and simply read the letter out loud.

Each sentence skimmed across the child's consciousness like a pebble the intervening seas had ripped from his grasp. Shoe scuffs against the tarmac outside broke the silence. It sank and yet it didn't sink in. He listened to older boys strut across the yard to play a game with a tiny ball hit with the hand against the walls of an enclosed square. It was called fives, but no one told him its rules. The ball stung his fingers, but it didn't hurt. It was not understanding the rules, and not knowing who or how to ask that hurt. He had tried his hardest to join in, but outsiders were at best tolerated, never accepted. Theirs was the world of Empire and Service, of Queen and Country, of Honour and of Fellowship. A hundred million light years from his own childhood in Biafra.

The ritual scarring of his cheeks three years earlier than his cousins to say 'You are Igbo'. The pained pride to be a man, not a boy, and the anguish that he must leave as a man, an Igbo Man, not yet eleven. He stared at the photographs that lined one panelled wall of Mr Wing-Collar's study. Layer upon layer of boys identical in uniforms since 1896. They were like the tribal masks the young men wore when their elders met. His fingers felt the ridges in the squared scars in each cheek. It sank in. They were all that remained of home. Its death lay beyond the understanding of those alien rows of boys.

Tears fell from Nigal Adtombwe's eyes like stones. He ducked Mr Congreave's arm, brushing under its tweed sleeve and the scent of aftershave, pushed open the door and ran. Past the dead statues, and outside to breathe, to search the sky for the faces he had known since birth. He wanted them to explain. To be there, with him, now. He needed his family to tell him how his family had disappeared and why they were dead. He had no one to hold.

*

John Tilt decided to take the wreath from the dark stranger's gloved fingers. It had been held out rather than offered directly.

Released from the wreath, the stranger removed his gloves to stare at his hands, toughened, made rough with physical work.

Tilt saw how the tailored coat covered a strongly built man, evidently fit and well. It made no sense. The words were a freakish mistake, the stranger had attended the wrong funeral. These things happen; grief only obeys its own time and calendar. The wind hurled grains of rain from the sunlit sky into the dark petals of the wreath. Tilt offered it back. Tears welled from the stranger's eyes to fall like river-washed boulders.

'I thought they would bury him,' he repeated inside silent mumbling.

Tilt watched the tears track across the squares of tribal markings. 'Sorry to say this, but you are quite sure you're at the right funeral?'

'Are you? We met over thirty years ago. How did you know him?'

The rain was just starting to rub between Tilt's neck and collar. He motioned to a patch of shelter under the entrance to the cemetery. The rain stopped in the wind.

'I didn't,' Tilt said. 'I never knew him. Not until he was dead.'

'Then why you are here? Except because of me,' the stranger replied. 'I killed him. I sandblasted him to death.'

He watched the colour fade from Tilt's face as it darkened to the hue of granite. The wreath dropped to the ground. Adtombwe let the other man hold out a laminated plastic ID card. He compared its photograph with reality. They were identical.

'I am arresting you on the suspicion of murder.' Detective Inspector Tilt's words shivered against the wind. 'You

109

retain the right to remain silent, but I should caution you that anything you fail to mention now, but employ in your defence at a later date, may be held in court against you. And anything you do say, may also be used in evidence.'

As if he were a blind man seeking guidance, John Tilt held onto the other man's elbow. He sensed he was about to be swallowed by an enormous monster. He knew there was no mistake. A creature who fed on death and misery. There was no escape.

Without realizing it they left the wreath where it had fallen against the crematorium wall. The city stopped; its noise hung in the air like dust in the half-light of a cathedral. The wind started to claw at the wreath, to strew its petals across time.

Sheffield City Police Authority   SPF 12b/(i)may87

Surname: **ADTOMBWE**

Christian or First Names: ~~**NIGEL**~~ **NIGAL**

D.O.B: **14.08.54**   Age: **43**

Sex: **Male**   Marital Status: **Single**

Dependants: **None**   Next of Kin: **None**

Nationality: **U.K Foreign National (Nigerian)**

Ethnicity: **IC3**

Religion: **None**

Employment: **Artist**

Current Address:

> **15 Dagnell Crescent**
> **Netherside**
> **Sheffield S14 2AP**

Previous Addresses (in last five years):

> **None**

Signed: *R G Mills*   Dated: **16 April 1998**

Name: **Ronald G Mills**
Rank & Number: **Sergeant / GA716**

Twelve

Nigal Adtombwe watched the white distemper flake from the wall opposite. The glue of a teabag gave an oily sheen to the UHT milk particles that flecked the surface of the stale drink in a stained melamine mug. It stuck to the lime green ledge nailed next to the narrow bed and screwed into the tiled floor. He lay on a crushed felt blanket, waiting for the iron spyhole to flick open, then shut on the quarter hour, its giant eye ready to chalk up the next mark on a board hidden outside.

Inside his head he tried to make a picture of this place in order to escape it. It had worked before. He tried to remember the number of marks he had heard being chalked up outside. He had no other means of counting time. Eleven or twelve seemed about right. They had taken away his watch but he had already lost track of events. Wallet, keys, loose change; he signed for them with his pen, and then they took that away with his name too. It didn't hurt. Belt, tie, shoe-laces, socks and hat, each pushed flat inside a thick square polythene bag. They watched his sheepish grin as his trousers' waistband collapsed to his hips. Adtombwe did not hitch them back up. They watched his lips' ceaseless silent mutterings.

They could take away whatever they liked. He'd not forget. He was not going to kill himself. He had killed already.

Two floors up Bill Naylor found John Tilt outside his office when he came back from lunch.

'Sir. Something urgent has cropped up.'

'In records?' DCI Naylor distinctly remembered signing the transfer memo.

'No sir. Here. The Reddlewood case.'

'The Redd – You'd better come in.'

The door seemed to pull Naylor into his office. As ever Tilt obeyed orders. He stood the other side of a bare desk while Naylor crumpled into its chair.

'I thought we'd closed the Reddlewood case weeks ago.'

'Yes sir. Ten days.'

DCI Naylor waited for DI Tilt to continue.

'That is why I went to the funeral. Of the victim.'

Tilt explained at a slow measured pace. He watched Naylor's slightly dazed eyes widen. The news just might sober him up enough to act effectively.

Naylor listened carefully, very carefully, but failed to understand, in particular Tilt's motives. The DCI also held himself to be a Christian, certainly not a diligent one, but he did not regularly attend the funerals of total strangers. It seemed a strange thing to do. Certainly not in the course of duty. Just being an ordinary copper was punishment enough. He wanted Tilt back in records.

'The case is still to be filed, inspector.'

No response. He watched Tilt speak to the window. The same dead voice and expressionless face that Jack Singleterry used in order to unsettle others. Tilt explained that the suspect, a Mr Nigal Adtombwe, had admitted to knowing the deceased thirty years ago. 'I arrested him on the suspicion of murder. He said he had committed it.'

Bill Naylor checked the calendar. April 16th, not 1st. Tilt didn't play tricks anyway. Too dull by half. The arrest was real enough. Their suspect had to be insane.

113

'You've contacted social services?'

'Yes, sir. There's no record of any client with that name in the last seven years. I've also spoken to the Nigerian Embassy. Mr Adtombwe holds dual nationality. No record of any relatives either here or abroad. Apart from renewing his passport they know nothing more either.'

Naylor splayed his fingers through his thinning hair. The lunatics should never have closed Shale Moor Hospital; now they were all out on the streets. It was bad enough with ordinary people.

'Just a moment, there were at least four of them.'

'Four sets of different bootprints, sir,' Tilt corrected. 'Just one vehicle.'

'Whatever. He must be mental.'

'Yes, sir.' Earlier at the custody desk Tilt had already made up his mind. He had requested the At Risk Register and placed the prisoner on it. The silent mutterings hadn't ceased.

'He might well be mentally ill, sir, but I think he did it. He knew the means of death. He knew about the sandblasting.'

It took about five seconds. Naylor's eyes widened in disbelief. He winced from the sharp pain inside his gut. They had closed the case. Left it unsolved, virtually on purpose in order to shove a cast-iron manhole cover over the mess of two botched investigations colliding with an almighty bang at Airport Van Hire. DCI Naylor had pulled out all the tricks he knew to save their collective arses and careers, not to mention a fair few special favours. The Stacy-Fisher gang had already been cautioned for the Reddlewood murder by the Manchester Met. This made things very difficult. Very difficult indeed.

'The arrest, inspector. Not a long while since?'

'Three hours, sir. It's in the book.'

It would be, thought Naylor.

Less than half a day for him to sort it before Singleterry found out. All for some half-crazed Nigerian. This were going to be hard work, bloody hard work. Singleterry wouldn't want to spend time proving some darkie innocent; he'd tell them they all had better things to do. Villains to nail, sod their colour. He certainly wouldn't want to admit the truth to the Serious Crime Squad up in Leeds. Not to DCS Birtels. She was black, Jack was racist, this was crazy. Singleterry would crucify everyone in sight. Fuck Christianity – why the hell did Tilt have to go and attend the funeral? The ordinary decent thing to do was always wrong.

'I'll interview the suspect,' the Chief Inspector said. 'With Sergeant Ashurst.'

'Very well, sir. What would you like me to do?'

'Go back to bloody records – no, phone this Atomboy's house.'

'I have, sir. While you were away. No reply. He does not appear to have a family.'

DCI Naylor didn't care. 'Visit it then. You'd better take someone. See who's left in pool.'

They needed to ask directions from a passer-by. Half the street signs in Netherside had disappeared, while the city A–Z had been ripped from the chain attaching it to the dashboard of the pool car. Not by the same thief.

DC Wilet drove off before Tilt could say thank you to a friendly pensioner outside a betting shop. She was sick of the job. After Airport Van Hire, word had gone round the canteen that she wasn't just a girlie, but a lezzie. Worse: Singleterry had intimated in that foul-breathed way of his that she'd be blamed for the cock-up between his section and the Serious Crime Squad from Leeds, for recklessly using her partner's car, not an official police vehicle. DC Wilet didn't want to say anything to anyone. And certainly not to DI Tilt, not now they were collectively known as Jesus and the Lezzie by all the plods and plonks. She wanted to cry.

Detective Inspector Tilt watched her slam their car door shut, just like every other police officer he knew.

The window frames of number 15 were still their original wood, top coat of gloss peeling away, instead of double-glazed uPVC. They made it look a little more old-fashioned, a little less kempt, almost more ordinary than its semi-detached neighbours. There was no one around, but Tilt watched for a twitch of net curtains up and down the street. They might need to ask the neighbours.

Wilet rushed ahead. Number 15 had no nets. She stepped up the worn drive. Weeds and moss indicated where the tarmac had decayed back to earth. Tilt pulled at her sleeve to ensure her shoes did not disturb a small pool of dead engine oil. As expected, no one responded to their knock, but the key turned in the lock as simply as it had been given to them. DI Tilt had thought a warrant would be required, but Mr Adtombwe agreed to their search without question.

They had informed their prisoner that they would return with a change of clothes and a toilet bag. Within his silent mumbles their prisoner nodded and shook his head, which they took as consent. Inside his own house he had nothing left to hide.

Tilt shut the door behind them softly. They had stepped into a different world.

Without a word they followed procedure: a preliminary examination of all the rooms before any further detailed work. Nothing seemed out of place. The dust on the mantelpieces of the two spare rooms upstairs demon-strated how Adtombwe lived alone, without regular visitors. Downstairs was also tidy, rather than neat. News-papers stacked in a pile, pot plants well watered but leaves left unpolished. Chair cushions flattened by use, not plumped up. The sitting room was spotless. An over-powering stench of air-freshener hit them as soon as they opened its door, making their eyes smart. The glosswork and windows were covered with its stickiness.

Wiping the air-freshener astringency from their eyes, they nearly missed the remains of a TV remote control left crushed into the carpet, tiny black shards of plastic embedded into its pile. There was no television set either, just a space above a video recorder. There was something else, too, something else missing. Each room seemed odd in a way neither of them could quite place. It hit Ruth Wilet first.

No ornaments, no pictures on the walls, no photographs on shelves or mantelpieces. The house was empty of them. No memorabilia, no family, school, graduation or wedding album shots, no works dos: a complete absence of recorded identity. Not even a small framed image of a child smiling gap-toothed at a camera. Perhaps they'd been taken down? No. No tell-tale lighter squares on the walls where pictures had once hung. Ruth Wilet felt cold, chilled. The body inside the empty building had lost its identity too.

Each window lacked curtains, just the old brass runners of previous households, no assured means to respect privacy. He's an artist, thought Tilt, as if this explained everything. But this house didn't need curtains: there was nothing in it to see. No pictures, no images, no TV – it was a place without memory. Tilt and Wilet thrust their hands deeper into their pockets, searching for something ordinary to hold onto. They wanted to open up the windows, to let some fresh air in, to dispel for ever whatever it was the air-freshener was hiding. John Tilt sneezed and Ruth Wilet smiled at something so ordinary, before they fixed themselves to return to the standard procedures of investigation.

The kitchen looked over a long narrow garden, laid entirely down to grass, cut but not trimmed at its edges. They discovered another sink in the pantry, installed quite recently. Darkroom, he explained in its red light's glow to DC Wilet's puzzled stare at the shelves of chemicals and print paper. He pointed to the thermostat and wall thermometer to tally with the bottles of colour developer and the professional enlarger, the drying rack and hangers. Yet Adtombwe dared not hang any pictures up outside this tiny windowless room.

DC Wilet went upstairs. DI Tilt washed his hands at the sink for no particular reason except they seemed to itch from the air-freshener. He let the tap run, cherishing the touch of cold water.

The bathroom toilet flushed and he waited for Wilet to come down. She carried a plain toilet bag, and asked the inspector to select a change of clothes before they left. At the far end of the kitchen was a door that led to the garage. None of the keys in Tilt's pocket fitted. Ruth Wilet opened the fridge to find a key nestling in the egg tray. A guess, she explained: her mother did the same in her house. From fridge to freezer kept in the garage. Some things are simple.

In the dark their hands fumbled round the doorway for a light switch. Tilt found it first. Mr Adtombwe's garage was tidy too. Normal, almost. Racks of tools, shelves of paints and cleansers, a hard broom next to a plastic dustbin. Virtually no clutter or mess stashed away out of sight and mind. A stout workbench with a vice and drill-stand blocked the up-and-over door. Wilet located another light switch. Four daylight lamps shone into the centre of the space. No dust. It had been kept pristine. Two industrial power points dangled from the roof. Their sockets stayed empty, ready for the tools to move from their racks.

Beneath the daylight lamps a strange sculpture waited as it had waited in darkness. One third snake, one third crocodile and one third bird. Its scales were shreds of old tyre, its body bits of cracked pallet. Claws tin, teeth glass and feathers carpet: broken bits of the city reunited with other bits of existence. Wire, welds, rivets, bolts and nails, tired and dull, alive only for this purpose. Crawl, slither or fly off. To scream in its own agony. Did any neighbours complain about the noise?

The creature was paralysed. It seemed unable to move, survive or die. Its eyes, empty spaces, stopped its visitors from moving. John Tilt started to understand where they were. Neither a workshop nor exhibition but something more basic, brutal. In an art gallery or studio suffering becomes art: both eternal, each safe. Within an artspace people may be affected but not hurt by what they feel. Here was different: the suffering had still to finish. The two police officers felt themselves being pulled into the belly of this creature. It seemed to live off their pain. Ruth Wilet needed to return to their car, to take care rushing along a diagonal of lighter-coloured tiles. Tilt held her hand for a moment. Together they had seen that the tribal markings on Nigal Adtombwe's face were also etched into the creature's metal cheeks. They were inside a model of blasting bay six.

On the workbench Tilt noticed a book he knew from somewhere else. In the art section of a bookshop somewhere . . . upstairs in Waterstone's, a poster of *The Prophetic Visions of William Blake*. Come closer, it ordered, and he obeyed until it hit him. Nigal Adtombwe had sculpted *The Flight of the Phoenix* that hung over the Hole in the Road down from the cathedral yard. He opened the book. To his fingertips the paper started to feel like the autopsy report. He leafed through the pages, then noticed a small Jiffy bag. His eyes traced a printed poem on the workbench next to the bag.

119

A DIVINE IMAGE

Cruelty has a Human Heart,
And Jealousy a Human Face;
Terror the Human Form Divine,
And Secrecy the Human Dress.

The Human Dress is forged Iron,
The Human Form a fiery Forge,
The Human Face a Furnace seal'd,
The Human Heart its hungry Gorge.

Someone had run a pencil underneath its first line. Tilt closed the book and let his fingers feel their way into the bag. The murderer was about to take them into blasting bay six.

The space inside the bag became the inside of a reptile egg, ready to hatch. The edges of a set of images brushed the tips of Tilt's fingers, a creature's first touch with the world outside. Inside its egg, its skin had already learnt to change colour. It waited to be exposed, recorded, a film of events and their causes. As it hatched outside the bag, the creature opened its eyes.

The detective inspector stared at a set of Polaroids ripped from a camera's black back. Their colours. Red, yellow and grey.

These photographs had witnessed the killing. One by one they gradually restored the naked flesh which sandblasting had taken away. The hands, the feet, the chest, the mouth, the genitals, the hair, the face and the eyes of the victim.

Thirteen

Inside the interview room Nigal Adtombwe waited for DS Ashurst and DCI Naylor to leave. The cassette tapes stopped at the end of their run inside the grey machine screwed to the wall a foot above the table. Sergeant Ashurst replaced them with a fresh pair according to procedure. Naylor checked his watch against the clock above Adtombwe's head. He glanced at the sergeant, who shrugged his shoulders. They pushed into limp air. Nobody moved their lips for a further five minutes.

Bill Naylor kicked the table to check the instrument needles of the grey machine. The needles jumped, nothing else did. Adtombwe stayed seated, a statue of stillness and silence. No nod, no shake of the head, no look away or twist of the body.

Fifteen minutes ago the detectives had finally stopped asking their questions, the same questions they had asked the moment Sergeant Ashurst had closed the interview room door behind them three hours earlier. Naylor was so tired of hearing nothing except air come from their suspect's lips that he wrote the questions down to help him concentrate on the task at hand. They had asked them over and over again.

Where was he three months ago, during the night of Saturday 24th January?

How did he know the man left to die inside the empty building?
What was his name?
Who else was involved? Their names?
How had they gained access?
What were their motives?

As soon as Adtombwe had seen Naylor his lips had clamped tight. Nigal Adtombwe said nothing. To them, to the tape recorder, to the walls. He had said nothing for three hours. Why? Why couldn't they think of any more questions to get him to talk? Why had he confessed to Tilt?

Tired haunches underneath the table ached with the cassette recorder's grey whirr. Nigal Adtombwe wiped his nostrils with a paper napkin they had served with their cold inedible food. Detective Sergeant Ashurst nudged the elbow of his chief inspector to check he didn't fall asleep. Bill Naylor kept his eyes shut. Somewhere in the past this seemed to have happened already. His memory failed to locate precisely where. He and another officer in this interview room, before tape recorders. He remembered his hands taking down a statement. A long time ago. That was all. The who, the what and the why had disappeared. It must have come to nothing, otherwise he would have remembered.

The detectives left the interview room dry-tongued and exhausted from having faced three hours of impenetrable silence. They could not wrench a sound out of a suspect who had already confessed to murder.

Why the wall of silence? No one lasted three hours. Fifteen minutes, half an hour, maybe an hour, hour and a half tops. Until the questions, the offers, the snide remarks and the direct threats aimed square at the back of the head twisted lips apart. The verbal jemmy worked every time. A nod of a head to the offer of a smoke and the suspects had started to talk. Sweet tea, a bacon buttie dripping tomato sauce, selected phone calls outside, soccer half-times, any one of these could lever a suspect, elbows on the table, open like a packet of cigarettes. It was still difficult, of course, hard for a blunt fingernail to lift up that tiny red flap on the cellophane wrapper of the smokes. Hard for them to take the first cigarette, so tightly squeezed in by the others. To pull them out, each easier than the last, offered up and smoked, until nothing remained in the packet. To be thrown away, crushed.

Then the hard part was over, finished with. Forget their No Smoking signs, there was always another packet. Each interview possessed the same pattern inside the smoke. Listen, give, evade, deny and lie, only to give a little more. Each fabrication was stretched, toyed with, nearly bought, then ruthlessly torn to shreds and stuffed straight down the throat of the suspect – who coughed and spluttered the regurgitation of another story inside the first. And the lies grew smaller and smaller inside another story, and another, and then another, until only the truth, to be presented in court, remained.

It took time – hours, days, a week or more. They knew how to wait after the first infinitesimal crack. The wait made Bill Naylor's satisfaction all the more pleasurable. He liked to be a slow, patient man. But before then, within the vacuum of silence, it was impossible for anyone to break a suspect down, to smoke out a confession. There was no smoke here, just bare emptiness. Even Singleterry would be reduced to impotence. His bare hatred would hold nothing to crush.

DCI Naylor shoved a memo back into its pigeon hole. Their suspect was not stoned. The MO's report showed no drugs other than a trace of a proprietary nasal decongestant, available without prescription. Naylor had more pressing duties. How to neutralize Mad Jack Singleterry for starters. Inside the station he had to find him a safe target to destroy. Adtombwe had already confessed. Perhaps that was the trick. He had nothing else left to lose.

John Tilt walked straight into Naylor's office without knocking and straight out again. Empty. Tilt remained stuffed full of anger. No one was around. Wawner had left to cover an early, Kirk gone off sick, Hughes was not yet due in court: a duty roster full of blanks. Sometimes it seemed easier to track down criminals than policemen. Their section struggled to manage either.

Ruth Wilet cautiously watched DI Tilt when he returned to their office. He searched the cupboards for a polythene evidence bag. The box of bags was empty too. He resisted the urge to slam shut the metal doors. No one had bothered to check, to restock after they took the last one. The detective inspector could not let go of the Polaroids.

'Let's interview the suspect, shall we, constable?'

Nigal Adtombwe recognized Tilt from the funeral. He heard rather than listened to the explanation of procedures and the introduction of the young woman. She placed his washbag on the table between them. They had visited his house. They had kept their word, and his keys. He wanted to nod his head in agreement but fear held his neck rigid. His lips started their mumbles again. He tried to stop them and failed. If he said nothing, they could not discover the truth. Could not. The young woman pressed the red and black keys to start the grey cassette recorder. They listened to the soft whirr of magnetic tape travel through spools and rollers. His lips twitched and jumped just as mechanically. He wanted to say why he was afraid; he was too afraid to say anything.

'Open it,' Tilt ordered. Anger laced his voice with violence. His hand pushed the washbag across the table. Adtombwe kept his own hands underneath, palms pushing upwards, scared that the detective inspector might hit him. Tilt was ready to. 'Open it!'

DC Wilet hurriedly explained to the cassette recorder that the suspect had received his washbag. The detective inspector frightened her. While Singleterry simply intimidated, Tilt seemed to shake the room and lock its door with fear. Ruth Wilet wanted to reach over and help Adtombwe undo the washbag's zipper. He seemed too innocent, yet the scarring on each side of his cheeks reminded her of the tyre marks caught in the snow between castings in Reddlewood's yard. She didn't understand what was going on. 'Open the bag,' she whispered. 'Do as the inspector says.' She wanted Tilt to calm down; eyes to blink and soften. They didn't.

The needles flicked to the sound of the zip. Adtombwe peered inside. They had packed everything, except a razor.

He felt the bristles of his chin. He needed to shave twice a day, though he rarely did. His fingers found the soft delicate skin below his Adam's apple and rested there. His entire face had been like that once, not as now, coarse and abrasive as brick. Nigal Adtombwe remembered the stroke of another man's hands across his face. Much older, in control, seeming to burnish the tight squares of Igbo markings until they seemed to burn through his cheeks and raze his homeland to oblivion. Ever since that touch, he had been trying to escape what had happened next.

A leather button from a jacket cuff had brushed his ear. A finger travelled along an eyebrow. It was a favour at school, a special favour to be allowed to watch the television. His eyes tried to watch black and white images move in and out of the screen. They didn't seem to be alive. The sound did not seem to match their motion, it was almost like a silent film. He needed to escape the ciné camera inside the room. He tried to shrink himself into the television set; very far away, yet close. He had to lean forward, then shrink and slink between its tiniest black and white dots behind the glass of the TV set. It would be safe there. Inside those faraway nearly invisible stars it was always safe. The leather-buttoned man and his touch could not reach in there. Only his voice stayed inside Nigal's head.

The fingers had reached the middle of his forehead and, gently, pushed him back. They returned along his eyebrow. He tried to keep his eyes on the screen, while the enormous hands felt the softness of his cheeks. This time they ignored the Igbo insignia. His teeth could sink themselves into the flesh of the palm, but he did not know how. He did not dare. Left alone, his lips started to mutter to themselves, to call out silently to the camera, telling its clockwork whirr to stop.

He failed to prevent the hands moving up his thighs, wrenching trouser material tight, pulling it as far as it would go underneath his haunches. He tried to lift himself away from the harshly padded settee and freshly shaven cheeks. To escape the hands that removed clothes. They demanded nothing except flesh. They had turned the two tight Igbo squares inside out, raw and hot, blood fluxed with fear.

Thirty-two years later he felt the bristles of his chin. It made sense, total sense. He had sandblasted someone to death. He could not be trusted to shave himself. Those were the rules.

'Keep looking!' Tilt ordered. Toothbrush and paste, a natural face sponge, shower gel, shampoo and conditioner, roll-on deodorant. The bag held the soapy-salty smell of the bathroom, the aroma of flesh in the midst of being cleaned.

He wanted a bath, a long, forever hot bath. He had always wanted a bath afterwards. Not straight away, but when he had managed to open his eyes he wanted an enormous hot bath, so wide and steamy the sides became cliffs a sea voyage away. Sheer, white enamel cliffs, too sheer to climb without a narrow twisted path that remained secret. His secret, alone. This is how he escaped; no one else could reach in or pull him out. This is how he had survived. Only then, a long time afterwards, did he dare try to scrub away the paper dry smell of aftershave. They were lucky to be allowed a bath each week. His body shivered uncontrollably however much he turned the hot tap to add to the near scalding waters of the enormous bath.

In the interview room, his fingertips brushed the squared edges of the Polaroids. Red, yellow and grey; he had wanted to record the colours to check what was happening. He removed the pile of photographs from the washbag. They knew everything. They knew nothing.

Nigal Adtombwe sat upright in the chair. They watched as his lips stopped their mutterings. One by one he took the Polaroids and laid them down in sequence across the table. He remembered there were twenty-four. He laid them down, face-up, deliberately angled towards the two police officers, as though they were cards in a slow game of patience, not a record of a murder. A rectangle of terror took shape. He was telling them what he had done. Once or twice he nearly made a mistake, but he placed this deck of images down in the right order of events. It was he who held their sequence, understood its purpose. It became a strange way to tell a fortune, starting with a naked life, whose fate they already knew. Blasting bay six was over. The sound of sand and shot eating flesh entered the interview room.

He was inviting them to play with the life of a man in late middle age, without clothes, or a chance. Despite his situation, the victim looked as though he did not expect to die. Features distinguished, if not quite handsome, blasted into skinless oblivion. One eye seemed bruised, reddened, marked from a recent blow or fall. In the next row it was just blood and bone.

Ruth Wilet found it as hard to tear her own eyes away as it was to look. She understood DI Tilt's anger once she felt it grow within herself – against Tilt as well for not telling her first. Only when Adtombwe's hands ended the laying of Polaroids did she accept that they had committed the damage inside each small square tile. She turned to the door but remained seated: she wanted to be sick but her stomach refused to retch.

'For the purposes of the tape,' John Tilt stated as evenly as he could, 'Mr Adtombwe has placed across the table a set of Polaroid photographs of the deceased taken during the deceased's death.' Adtombwe stared at the sequence of squares and said nothing: his lips started to shape their meaningless mumbles. 'They were discovered by the arresting officer at the home of Mr Adtombwe.'

They looked so different from the detailed shots in the post-mortem report. These were alive.

Tilt wanted to sweep them from the table, and in the same motion smash his fist into Adtombwe's face, obliterate it with a sandblaster. Shaken by the force of his anger, he took a step back, trying to discard his emotions like a pile of clothes left out to wash. They stayed with him alongside the heavy scent of charred abraded flesh.

John Tilt spoke slowly. 'You told me you killed him.'

The muttering did not stop.

'You said nothing to my colleagues. Not one word.'

Nigal Adtombwe held his hand over his mouth. It was the only way he knew how to hold back the past, gag their voices. His lips finally let him speak. 'No,' he agreed, with care. He hardly knew Tilt but was too scared to lose him. 'No, I did not. It's not safe to.'

They had taken away his tie, belt and shoelaces. Thirty-two years ago at the wrong end of a junior dormitory corridor they had found a boy hanging by his dressing-gown cord from the wooden door frames to the toilets. Door frames without doors – they couldn't even pass water in private. Everyone heard the cleaner's scream. A broken-backed howl from another world. Eerie in a place without mothers, an institution which banned and punished femininity. Nigal Adtombwe had prayed it would never happen. In the night he had listened to the rustle of bedclothes pulled back slowly, the soft pad of bare feet lightly touching bare floorboards opposite. They had learnt to tread cautiously, feel their way into darkness, to break the rules. The Cutlers' School forbade full bladders at night. The prohibition fostered discipline.

In their dorm Nigal had waited. His fingertips counted the ridges in his Igbo cheeks. Fifteen, perhaps twenty minutes passed. The rest of his face was still soft, young, untouched. He listened carefully but perhaps not carefully enough. He heard footsteps, heavier, not the soft pad of bare feet coming back. He thought he recognized them. Something was wrong. The bed opposite still looked empty. He traced their secret path, went to open the dormitory door, to lever it up by its bakelite handle to be sure it did not screech against the wooden floor. His hand missed the handle. The door was wide open; the boy had not returned. Nigal went to look. He had to: Jez was his closest friend.

Hands against the wall, he stepped down the dark corridor towards the faint light that the moon managed to sneak past the washroom's windows. This was against school rules. His fingers felt for the door at the far end of the passage. It was closed. Slowly he twisted it open. This door swung freely. They had sawn six inches away from its bottom to help the cleaner's mop.

He wanted to be sick, he wanted to scream. He stood still, then walked across the stone-tiled floor, their bleak, shadowy diagonals. He stubbed his toe on an upturned zinc mop bucket and froze at the near shriek it made. He wanted to stop the shadow of his friend swinging from a quarter moon. His hands held the legs, waist, arms, chest as far as he could reach on tiptoe. Underneath the pyjamas the flesh felt as cold as the stone floor. The stench of fresh urine and faeces pooled beneath the body struggled to overcome the ingrained decades of cheap disinfectant. There was nothing he could do. He went back the way Jez should have returned, and waited for the night to disappear. He didn't want to think about how Jez had died.

It had to happen. The cleaner's scream woke the rest of the dorm. He had not dared to sleep. His best friend was dead, hanging by a dressing-gown cord at the far end of the corridor, and suddenly his head was full of voices – family, homeland speaking at the same time as the boys and teachers here. He tried to talk back, to tell them all to be quiet, but they wouldn't listen. It was driving him mad. Instead he turned over his pillow to hide the tears that had soaked into the stuffing. He heard the voices tell him what to do. He'd say nothing to the teachers.

'Is it safe to speak now?' Tilt demanded. 'For the purposes of the tape Mr Adtombwe keeps muttering to himself. Can you give us, write down, the names of the others involved? Mr Adtombwe declines to reply. Very well, the man in these photographs: who is he? You must know. What is his name?' They waited a few further minutes for a response. 'Interview suspended. Mr Adtombwe continues to remain silent.'

The tape recorder clicked and the policeman removed the cassettes. It was safe now, the voices told Nigal Adtombwe, he didn't have to talk. He was not afraid to say who and why he had killed, state his name after all these years, but he could not tell them. Not because of the voices, which would never go away. They had made him into this man who did not want to hurt anyone else ever again.

Fourteen

It seemed as if nothing had happened. DI Tilt walked back down Carrdyke Lane to stop outside the empty Reddlewood building. Nearly three months had passed. He pulled up the collar of his coat.

The wind had scuffed an empty plastic cup into a gap behind a cracked drainpipe. The cardboard refreshment tray had squelched itself into the wet cobbles. Its indent in the snow had long since disappeared with the snow and the sector car it had sat on. The slam of scene of crime's van doors was silent, missing. Tyre tracks in the old snow, topped up with a fresh fall, were gone, for ever. Time had ripped the incident tapes stretched across the yard. The detective inspector grasped a blue and white knot tied to nothing. Perhaps the foundry castings abandoned outside were a little rustier, but the empty building remained the same, Reddlewood Industrial Finishers still visible in the grain of the wooden signboard above the main entrance, where the wind and rain had worn away the paint of the lettering long ago. It seemed that it had never happened.

John Tilt stepped across the half-open door. Splintered screwholes halfway up its jamb marked the missing padlock hasp. It still showed how it had been jemmied open to unlock the fusty smell of rust, oil, warped furniture and faded paperwork. Two or three times, judging from the hasp's indentations in the paint. He stepped up the

131

gantry stairs, still keeping to one side, careful not to obscure the steps of those before him. There had been prints of four. But not four different people. DI Tilt realized that Adtombwe had visited ahead of the murder, to plan the event. He stared down at the six blasting bays. Their silent compressors, sand and shot agitators, drums of coolant emulsion and hydraulic taps.

It made no sense. A killer might attend the funeral of his victim, just to allay suspicions, but not to give himself up. Standard operational procedure was to delay the funeral until investigations were complete. The funeral had forced Adtombwe and himself together. They had only solved the case by declaring the case closed. Tilt half-smiled at the breakthrough that irony had lent them.

Irony was rust on the surface. Burial of the case had led to the funeral, where John Tilt had tripped over the murderer by accident. An accident of faith. Suppose he had failed to attend the funeral?

Back at the station Detective Superintendent Singleterry had told DCI Naylor to keep DI Tilt and DC Wilet on as the interview team. They had to bury the real case completely and Singleterry wanted to make sure it stayed that way. Jesus and the Lezzie were bound to screw up, he calculated. No bottle. This time Tilt kept his head down. He knew he had the bottle to prove Singleterry wrong.

Adtombwe must have visited the cemetery day after day to be certain of seeing his victim leave this earth. Tilt remembered the murderer's reason for coming – 'I had to make sure he was dead' – and wondered if this wasn't the reason he himself had returned to the crime scene.

Holding onto the rusting handrail, he walked down the gantry steps in search of a light switch. He turned round sharply. No one there except the sense of the murderer, a breath down his neck. But Nigal Atombwe was locked up back at the station.

The light bulbs failed to respond. Tilt tried again. His broken thumbnail snagged against the dead switch: they were disconnected from the city. He no longer spoke about the case to his wife; they were still struggling to remain on speaking terms. She'd said he had become obsessed, and he knew she was right but could do little about it, not even confess to her. It would be a betrayal of attraction, a loss of his credibility. It didn't stop him from wanting to see the case through to its end, at whatever cost to them all. He needed to understand its cause, whatever the dangers. From the Polaroids he couldn't remember the victim's face. The detective inspector had to persuade the murderer to do one thing. The dead man lived inside the murderer's head. Tilt needed the help of Nigal Adtombwe to take them there.

He wanted to reverse time. Let its tender breeze unscuff a plastic cup or discarded wreath to unclose the crematorium's narrow doors and threadbare sombre drapes, then pull back a plain unnamed coffin from the incinerator. A hammer's claw would unnail its simple lid, and practised hands raise mutilated flesh, then heal the ravages of post-mortem examination. Turn around each X-ray plate. Guide with a wave of the arm an ambulance from the morgue to reverse back up a cobbled yard. Help stretcher the body through a half-open door and up gantry steps. Undial telephone numbers and radio messages. Retract ink from the notebook page and return words to more innocent minds. Let weather beacons lift snow from the cold earth and untie its chill. Then watch others go their way before they arrive. Reverse the night, unkink its rivers: banish the deed to seek its cause.

Dispel the close-to-sweet smell of sandblasted blood within this empty space. Lift and replace every gossamer of skin found strewn on gloves, visors and floor. Restore their broken tone. Invert process: turn inside out the steel finishing tools, reverse the power of the three-phase motors, compressors and abrasive agitator. Breathe back each tiny piece of embedded aggregate that pulped the corpse into the colour of night. Switch these machines to respirate death itself. Loosen the knots in the blue nylon rope that held the victim to the chair. Let him regain colour, senses, sight and life itself. Match oblivion with identity, unjemmy a padlock and let a man go free.

Into a city where rivers disappear.

Fifteen

Green-yellow electric light kidnapped the dawn. Nigal Adtombwe heard the spyhole cover slam. Underneath the blanket his hands held his haunches. It helped him believe it was safe to fall asleep. It helped him to imagine he might be able to escape. It helped as it failed, always. The room closed in. Inside his memory two enormous hands circled his neck, their fingers teasing out twisted hair behind his ears. They seemed to bury him. A large breath rushed to cover their touch, lips to his skin, fingers pressed into his flesh. He curled himself tighter. Smaller. Too frightened to push away the hands of a monster that robbed sleep from this cold, tired world.

Thirty-two years ago, two police cars and one ambulance raced to the Cutlers' School. Their alarm bells rang in the ears of the boys, who crowded to stick their heads out of their dormitory windows. The drivers squeezed their vehicles into the fives court outside the prep school house, line abreast, parallel to the markings. Pyjama-topped, short-back-and-sided, the row of schoolboys above clocked the cop cars, Zephyr and Westminster, quick and shrill, and the slower ambulance, Commer 30 cwt. The slam of their doors and heavy-booted dash of their occupants up the service steps sounded precisely the same.

The boys kept their heads stuck out of the dormitory windows. *Tabula rasa* upon entry, their minds fast became a fives court of symbols, designed to steer education clear from life. Latin and Greek were exercises in erudition in order to exorcize hurt, joy and pain. Two police cars, one ambulance – their ringing bells were hardly a problem compared to the translation of Herodotus, or the derivation of pl without a slide-rule. They soon had answers to everything.

Food poisoning: naughty Porky Johnston had managed to get his head stuck in the tuckshop refrigerator, then tried to eat his way out. Porky Johnston was there to deny it.
Theft: Porks had eaten the refrigerator as well.
Mental cruelty: the fridge had been empty.
Arson: Crim Williams tried to burn down the library to skive maths prep.
Heroism: the Crim had succeeded. Alas, theorem disproved. No fire engines. (ERF or Foden.)

In Nigal Adtombwe's dormitory they knew better, Jez's empty bed obvious to all. In his own bed Nigal Adtombwe crammed his pillow over his ears.

The head of dorm swaggered in. 'Away from the windows, Green Three. Hands off cocks, on with socks. And use Reds' bogs. Now.' No one moved. Heavy boots thumped up the back stairs; their head of dorm stopped twirling the tasselled end of his dressing-gown cord. 'Now!'

The neat line of boys disintegrated into children isolated from their parents and each other. Nigal heard the boots hammer into the tiles of the washroom floor. Tiles that had been ice-cold to his own feet. They stopped. They had discovered the body.

Fewer than twenty minutes ago these boys had heard the cleaner's scream and said nothing. Less alive now, the

136

scream still echoed inside their heads. A fives ball that struck the limits of their consciousness. They had long since learnt how to duck pain and skive reality. They waited for the ball to stop rebounding. No one dared touch it, or hit it with their fist, pick it up with tingling fingers. Boots clumped the body down empty stairs, vehicle doors slammed, engines revved and bells rang to signal the early morning run. In the dorm they already knew the rules: do not play with people from beyond the fives court.

Nigal knew why they had barred and bolted the washroom door. Nigal knew how the bed opposite remained slept in but empty last night. Only Nigal. He did not want to find out what had happened. Time needed to go back on its word to a few seconds before lights-out when they had shared a quick whispered goodnight and God bless. Jez had been alive then.

They had been best friends. He had discovered the body.

He waited for the rest of Green Three to tumble down for their run before breakfast. Inside, he tried to practise laughing with their jibes. Somehow he'd find a way to mumble along: he'd have to. He'd dress himself in the same uniform as the others, do what they did. Show some discipline. Anything to skive pain and reality. What else could he do? But not yet.

He stepped across the empty room, as carefully as his bare feet had stepped across darkness. Eyes closed, fingers touched a tousled sheet. A slow outline traced a sleeping child within its last folds. Jez, he whispered between mumbles. Jez, rise and shine. He wanted to bring him back, back here, back to life. To touch, hold hands as they had done before. He wanted to see him again. His Jez Rose.

He had, swinging from the moon. Dead, ready for the cleaner's scream.

He cried and cried into the empty pillow until he heard

matron's soft shoes patter up the final flight of stairs. The duty snide had spotted a second empty space midway down the long table, disgusting snouts in their troughs of swill.

Nigal Adtombwe had decided to tell the police. Only he did not know how to without breaking the rules.

Peter Congreave waited for the milk to cool the tea that had been poured into his cup. He noted the two policemen did not bother. They demanded an interview with each boy in Rose's dormitory. Inevitable, he supposed, but it would make it even harder to hush this up.

Somerville would be apoplectic about the damage to Cutlers' reputation. There'd be self-righteous comments about all the years he'd been in charge, how never had such an unfortunate incident been allowed to mar his years of service, and barely more than a decade since the governors had seen fit to establish the prep school, a mere five years into his, Congreave's, tenure of its headship, he had allowed this to happen. Well, he could handle Somerville. At least he was not required to meet distraught parents.

'We have to, sir. It's for the record,' the policeman taking notes added, quite unnecessarily in Congreave's opinion. Well, they would have to do something and they could hardly travel to the RAF base in Nicosia to interview Squadron Leader Rose and his wife. He'd sit in on all the interviews, so nothing untoward would be said.

They asked if he knew of any reason why the boy may have taken his own life. None whatsoever, the headmaster replied. 'I'll arrange for the boys to be brought here, constable, as soon as they've finished their breakfast. If you'd be so good as to wait.'

'Sergeant,' his colleague corrected, settling his trilby on his lap. 'Thank you, sir.'

Nigal Adtombwe shook or nodded his head to each routine question. The Cutlers' had taught him how to give the answers that were expected of him. He did not need to say how he had discovered his friend hanging from the frame of the toilet door, the quarter moon, the knot tied in the dressing-gown cord. He wanted to, but dared not mumble. He nearly asked them if he could see the dead boy, but was too scared they might ask why and he'd start to stutter and mumble instead. He waited for their next question.

'He were your friend?' The shorter of the two policemen repeated the question. The prep school headmaster sniffed at its grammar. 'He were your friend, Nigel?'

'Nigal,' corrected his headmaster. A common enough error; he had committed the same mistake on first meeting the child. 'Please answer their questions, Nigal. Yes, they were friends, as you said, sergeant.'

Nigal said nothing.

'Thank you, Mr Congreave. It's detective sergeant,' corrected the policeman at the window. Stuck-up pricks, he thought. For tuppence he'd show 'em who's boss. They watched him lean over the fives court.

'Nigel – Nigal, we all know this were – was – a terrible thing to have happened, but can you think of any reason why Jeremy might've –' With his notebook the other detective sheathed back the words 'topped 'imsel''. His colleague waited for him to get on with it. 'Any reason why this might have occurred,' concluded Detective Sergeant Notebook. 'Anything unusual or untoward you remember your friend might have said, or done? Take your time.'

'Jeremy Rose was a quiet boy,' the headmaster explained eventually. 'Serious, but not morose.'

He nearly stood up at the far end of the table, to separate, protect young Adtombwe from the two detectives. 'Someone rather like Nigal here.' Expressed with a show of an open hand and an understated smile. 'Perhaps that's why they were such good friends to each other, sergeant. This is most upsetting to us all, especially poor Nigal. I do not think . . .' The smile disappeared. 'It is sad as it is inexplicable. Tragedy always is.'

The detective sergeant's notebook was already shut. It contained the death. They were free to leave the tragedy.

Nigal watched his headmaster usher the policemen from his study. The same slight flick of the hand that dismissed a lower junior from his presence. It was funny how Mr Congreave now referred to his closest friend as 'Jeremy Rose'. Alive every teacher called, no, *had* called him Rose, or Rose, J. And just very occasionally, Jeremy. But never Jeremy Rose. Nigal had started to realize how this place worked; what made it tick. The Cutlers' School took their real names away, to be replaced by half a name, Smith or Smith Minor, or a nickname, the Crim or Porks. They never got their names back till they left or were dead.

Including their teachers: *Mr* Somerville, *Mr* Congreave. For all their pedigree and cramming of facts, it meant they were never complete inside this school. Never allowed to become whole. Rather like the quip in the Jennings that he and Jez had read over the summer holidays. 'I'm not a complete idiot,' a boy protests to his tormentor. 'Why? Which bit is missing?' They laughed but it wasn't that funny. Nobody was allowed to be whole at the Cutlers'. Not even their teachers. They all had bits missing.

It was strange, obeying strange orders in a strange way in a strange land like this. Funny strange, not funny ha-ha. It seemed to make sense to mumble. It was like the proper way to tie up shoelaces. It hid the bits that were missing. Jez would never be Jez again. Now and for ever it was to be 'Jeremy Rose', each letter tooled into a headstone of memories. Nigal Adtombwe had tried hard to forget the names of his own family. Far too many bits were missing. Lost.

Heeding orders helped him. He was growing to like the Cutlers' clear-cut world of titles and tasks, each under-lined, defined by their own special fives court logic. He mapped it out to protect himself. He relished taking a ruler and scoring a line underneath the title of a task and another line across the page at its end. It scarcely mattered what he put down on paper in between – largely copied from the board anyway. It helped confine his family to page 17 of their atlas: a dot somewhere on a map at 1:12,000,000 scale. It helped him to bury them.

In the margins of last term's rough jotters he had stopped doodling designs of Igbo markings. If it wasn't allowed, he might get caught. He had learnt to draw, which meant he could start again. To create a fresh world on a blank sheet of paper. It would be better than before.

But at lights-out, tears of stone fell from the child's eyes into the dark within every night. In the space between sleep and dreams they rolled faster and faster down a steep hill to plummet over a cliff. The stones smashed into the sea, breaking themselves apart against the waves. Strange creatures swam out of their fragments, and he had learnt to draw them inside his head, then on paper, and finally carve and fabricate them into sculpture.

Thirty-two years later the police had interviewed his neighbours:

'Not to speak to. Kept himself to himself. We all do, don't we? Never had any visitors, mind.'

'Sorry. Busy. It's in the post.'

'Been here years. No trouble. Why? What's he done?'

'I spoke to him once. He's got this sort of workshop in garage, like. Weird it is. He's not making anything that makes sense. Anyway, it were Christmas Day and tyre's jiggered. Jacking point's rusted right through – fixed now for MOT, officer – so I asks him if he's a jack I can borrow. Very helpful, he were. Very helpful. All on his own. Vickie asked him in for a drink, it were Christmas, but he said no. Nowt else really.'

'About time. He's one of them. You know – a racialist. Tell that big black gorilla to go back to bleeding Banana Land where he belongs. We don't want his sort round here, do we, George. George?'

'Our lad's not here. We don't know where he is, and if we did, we wouldn't have to tell you. Oh, number 15 across the way – you should have said. Needs to mow his lawn.'

'Only just moved in. Can't help you, mate.'

'Nice bloke. Artist, isn't he? Arthur used to work nights and asked if he could keep it down during the day, being next door. You know what it's like, you need your sleep. He apologized, said he didn't know, and whenever our Arthur were on lates, he kept his word and the noise right down. Never said much but you knew he cared. He asked if there was anything he could do when Arthur were first took poorly. Wouldn't hurt a flea. Not like some round here. A gentle man. You give him our best. Jean and Arthur.'

'No. Very little mail. This might interest you. I deliver the Crescent come eleven. Since New Year he's not been working in that garage. Always used to. Otherwise you wouldn't know he were here.'

'Strange sort. How do you describe it? He always looks lost. Bumping into things that aren't there. Has he had a stroke with that twitching of the lips he's got?'

John Tilt visited the City Gallery. Ms Tuille cleared a space among the framed canvases for the detective inspector's chair. 'Sorry. No one has time to file things,' she said, 'but pictures are that much – larger. Coffee, inspector? Tea?'

'No, thank you, Ms Tuille.'

'Imogen.'

They were about the same age. They both wore suits, hers a rather bright blue haute couture. John Tilt wondered how many visitors she received at work. Rather more than he did. 'You've come about the graffiti.'

'Graffiti, Ms Tuille?'

'Graffiti, inspector,' she repeated with some asperity. 'All over *The Flight of the Phoenix*, above the Hole in the Road.'

Tilt half-nodded his head. He remembered the crane that had manoeuvred it into place as he had left Waterstone's a few weeks earlier. He remembered the work in Adtombwe's garage. The envelope of Polaroids left with the book of Blake's *Prophetic Visions*.

'Last Monday I contacted the central police station. If I rang once, I rang a hundred times – are you listening to me, inspector? Someone has spraycanned it. Not just someone.' Imogen Tuille spoke as though she was on stage. As she paused for effect, Tilt noticed she wore make-up to match. 'You know exactly who it is. It is the Mark of Zorro! You don't seem to be interested in this, do you? I did think it rather strange that they'd send a detective inspector, but then you seem more fussed over drunks peeing in the streets at midnight.'

'Operation Blue Flush was not my responsibility, Ms Tuille. I will pursue your enquiry about the graffiti when I return to the station.'

'Then why are you here?'

'We're more interested in the sculptor.'

'Nigal Adtombwe. You should've said. What's he done? Is he all right?'

She watched Tilt pause before informing her that Adtombwe was assisting them with their enquiries. It was clear everything was not all right.

143

'We'd like to know a little more about his background. We thought you might be able to help.'

'Did you? He's not too many friends, has he?'

'No. We don't think he has. How long have you known him?'

Imogen Tuille wondered what could have happened. Her mind drew a blank.

'Ten, fifteen years. Since I came to the gallery. He's lived here a lot longer. Went to the Cutlers'.'

'Really?'

From her voice alone DI Tilt had realized that she was public school too. Short rather than petite. He could imagine how duty desk had dealt with her phone calls.

'Then the Slade for his foundation, the Royal College. A small but good round of exhibitions and commissions, here and there. Not many. The work's excellent, but people seem to find him . . . distant. No need to make notes, it's in his résumé. I'll give you a copy when we're finished.'

'Of course – thank you.'

'You could have borrowed some of his paintings too, except the council cut our picture lending service some time ago. Pity. Then again sculpture is his medium. You won't find much of his work on display.'

'He did *The Flight of the Phoenix*.'

'Only because I championed him. We had to fight hard to get him the commission, then that wretched airport has to go belly up. Being black hardly helps, but as a policeman you'd know all about that.' Tilt let this pass: he knew he was being tested. 'He deserves to be better known. Nigal's not exactly a Damien Hirst when it comes to selling himself – and I suppose I'm no Charles Saachi.'

Tilt thought of Nigal's neighbours. They seemed hardly aware of his work. 'How well do you know him, Ms Tuille?'

She stared at the canvases as though they held the

144

answer. John Tilt wondered why she wore just a little too much make-up. Perhaps a little too much was just right in a grey city like this, full of grey people more like himself than her.

'I'm not quite sure – Nigal must be a difficult person to get to know well. His thought patterns seem, rather, well, unusual, don't you think?'

'I couldn't say, Ms Tuille.' He twisted his finger underneath the rubber band around his notebook. 'When did you last speak to him?'

'Let's see. Before Christmas? Yes, before Christmas. We had arranged to transfer *The Flight* from the airport site. I wanted him at the unveiling. He never came. Oh yes, last month Sheffield College contacted me – they'd like him to teach some photography, part-time. If I said it to him once, I said it to him a thousand times. "Make yourself known, and you wouldn't have to do this tiresome lecturing. You're a sculptor, Nigal." But I think he prefers anonymity. Has he disappeared, inspector?'

'No. Not exactly.'

'Then there's something you don't want to tell me.'

'There is. What will happen to the sculpture?'

'*The Flight*? After we somehow pay for the removal of the graffiti? Scrap, I dare say, before too long, if people keep complaining about it. It's scarcely ironic. "Some cities love their antiquities. Sheffield has few to boast of, and therefore treats them with scorn. Some day it will regret it." Not mine, I'm afraid. The *Sheffield Daily Independent*, 1906. You would not know the battles I've had here. All they want are fountains and animated clocks, glorified garden gnomes, nothing to challenge and excite. The Mark of Zorro will probably outlast us all. Not that Nigal will probably mind: whoever sees his work is incidental to him. He's a recluse. That résumé.'

Imogen Tuille chasséed her way through to another table

of papers to give him a copy of the two-page resumé. It was prefaced by the excerpt from *The Divine Image* they had found in Adtombwe's garage studio, 'Cruelty has a Human Heart'.

'Thank you. He's like Blake, isn't he?'

'Yes, he is. Pursued by visions.' She laughed. 'You've surprised me, inspector. I didn't think the police had time for the arts.'

'No. We're far too busy trying to stamp out graffiti.'

Imogen Tuille walked the detective inspector back through the corridors behind the public gallery. She asked Tilt to pass on her best to Nigal Adtombwe, and he realized she meant it.

Three days after the ambulance had taken the body of Jeremy Rose away from the Cutlers' School, Adtombwe, N. had decided to see his headmaster. 'Please, sir, may I attend the funeral?'

Mr Congreave did not say yes, Mr Congreave did not say no. He would have to discuss it with the family of the deceased. They were upset. Inconsolable. Mr Congreave stared down at their feet. 'As we speak, the RAF are flying Squadron Leader and Mrs Rose home from Cyprus. Leave it with me.'

He left it with Mr Congreave. Three days later the great and glorious headmaster of the senior school, Bottleneck Somerville, addressed the prep school assembly.

'The funeral of Jeremy Rose took place last Sunday at their family church near Warminster. Mr Congreave represented School.'

It came across as the result of a distant rugby or fives fixture.

Nigal Adtombwe hammered into Mr Congreave's study. 'You said,' he wailed, 'you said, you said. *You said.*'

Congreave waited for Adtombwe's sobs to diminish, his

146

wrath to weaken. 'Control yourself, Nigal Adtombwe,' he said at last, using his whole name. 'We don't want to see you upset like this.' He sniffed a little himself. It was difficult to be clear. 'Pretend it never happened,' he whispered.

Adtombwe felt a hand rest across his shoulder, protecting, holding him back. As he turned to leave, he felt the thumb of his headmaster run across the back of his neck, a ruler underlining a task. Fingers teased out twisted hair behind his ears.

'Call me Peter,' the voice ordered. He closed his eyes; he knew he had to stay. Slowly he had started to realize why Jez had wanted to kill himself. The study door opened into his cell.

'Where are his clothes?'

Tilt had decided abrupt tactics might jerk Adtombwe to give up details. He found he could only control his anger with impatience. Suddenly he had wanted to finish the case, had to know what had happened. Ruth Wilet felt her own fingers tense around her thumb. In front of her eyes John Tilt was starting to change into Jack Singleterry. It worked. No more silent mutterings.

'Clothes?' their prisoner repeated.

'Yes, clothes,' Tilt snapped. 'The forensic report demonstrates your victim was naked when you – What did you do with the clothes?'

'I gave them away. Soaked them in Bio-tex, dry-cleaned them at a launderette and gave them away. A charity shop. Near the university.'

'When? We can check the shop and launderettes.'

'A week or so later, I can't remember. I did not know what else to do. I did not stop to think anyone would want them. The wireless said you'd fished a body out of the river.'

It just about made sense.

'Go on.' Tilt and Wilet waited. 'Tell us who you were with that night.'

'Sorry. S-s-s-sorry. I can't.'

'Don't be sorry. Tell us!' snapped John Tilt. It was crazy. They still didn't know the name of the victim, and now more unknown people were walking round Sheffield wearing the victim's clothes. 'We have the Polaroids. Forensics have found particle traces at your home which match the abrasives found in the body. There's glue from discarded visors on your gloves, blood from the victim. Sooner or later we're sure to find someone who'll recognize the face you removed from the body. Delay is pointless. Tell us the name of the man you killed.'

'Sorry. I can't. I can't. I can't. I can't –'

The prisoner stopped his chant just as the detective inspector readied a right hand to slap him, hard.

'Why not? You do happen to know the name of this person you happened to sandblast to death.'

'Yes. No. I can't tell you. I can't –'

Tilt's right arm twitched. Ruth Wilet poured water into a glass. The recording needles shuddered with the tumble from the jug. It seemed to calm the air.

'Right, Mr Adtombwe,' she said, pushing across the glass. 'Who else is involved?'

'No one.'

'No one?' The prisoner had confirmed the DI's reckoning in the empty building. A single vehicle driven by a single perpetrator.

'No one. Not now.'

'No one else is involved?' Tilt repeated.

Adtombwe said nothing. He alone had planned and executed the event.

'Then why did you take the Polaroids?'

Their prisoner's lips started to jerk before his hands could hide them.

148

'You did take them?'

Adtombwe managed to nod his head.

'Why?'

'I can't tell you,' Adtombwe wailed. 'I can't –'

'All right,' whispered DC Wilet. 'Let's leave it. Please?'

The needles on the tape recorder rested upon their silence.

'Can you say why you attended the funeral?'

The two men stared at each other.

'I've already told you,' Nigal Adtombwe whispered back. 'I had to make sure he was dead.'

Ruth Wilet bit down on her own hand. Inside her head the Polaroids and blasting bay six merged into one. She finally dared to close her eyes. How could anyone who had sandblasted someone to death then attend their funeral to determine they weren't still alive? It didn't make sense.

Tilt walked to the far end of the room. They were getting closer to the truth. 'You did not know when the funeral was.'

'It didn't matter,' Adtombwe replied just as slowly. 'Every day I went to the cemetery. Otherwise I'd never have known if he were dead.'

'Despite the Polaroids?'

'Because of them. He is dead, isn't he?'

Their prisoner's hand reached out for the glass of water. It spilled across the table. Accidents happen, murders never end.

'Please help.'

John Tilt watched Ruth Wilet nearly rest a hand over their prisoner's. He was still living this murder.

'Mr Adtombwe. This is the last question for now. Who are you trying to protect?'

There were no pictures in his home. No framed photographs of relatives, friends and their children. No clear memories. No letters, bills, junk mail even. No art.

149

Mr Adtombwe lived entirely on his own. The world seemed to have left him that way.

'Can't you see? The people he knew.'

Three weeks after the funeral of his friend Jez Rose, Nigal Adtombwe had walked down the school drive and taken the bus straight to Sheffield city police station. He did not know what to say: telling them the reason why Jez had died would never bring him back.

The electric light disappeared, the spyhole cover slammed and two enormous hands circled his neck. Beneath a blanket of choked mumbles his own hands still held his haunches tight. He and the strange creature writhed in agony. The past swallowed everything.

Sixteen

Neither did John Tilt sleep that night. He did not want to until he had solved the case. His family had made it plain they hated him for becoming so much more distant since the funeral, but he didn't care. He needed to find out who Nigal Adtombwe had killed. Who cared if it was an obsession? It was his duty.

He left for work hours before anyone else woke up, tidying up his bedding from their settee and taking his washbag with him. He didn't want to disturb his family any more than he had to. A carton of orange juice spilled onto the floor as he gently opened the fridge door. How many times had he told their children to put things away more carefully? Ease up, chill out, get off our case, Dad, they protested, but he refused. They seemed to be doing it to spite him. His wife failed to back him up. I can't remember why we married, she explained. Her husband said nothing, but he couldn't remember either. He couldn't see a reason for having kids or doing anything at home. Mopping up the spilled juice, he remembered the stickiness of hydraulic fluid in blasting bay six. He couldn't remember how life was before then.

Electric razor buzzing in the station washroom mirror, he saw the Polaroid image of the victim's face pristine before death. Silver grey hair, distinguished features, almost an actor's face, as though make-up had masked any features out of character. Never boyish, now lines ran down each side of the nose to the ends of precisely drawn lips: a portrait ready to slide into the folds of time. No nicks or marks, skin just starting to harden and crease into old age as wrinkles gathered around the mouth as well as the eyes. He had a presence and stature that seemed to ignore time, while the blow that had bruised an eye left its gaze more assured – or was that make-up too? He appeared as calm and as close as someone bent back in a barber's chair ready for a wet razor to remove bristles and lather. John Tilt could nearly smell the aftershave as it merged with the air freshener in the sitting room of 15 Dagnell Crescent.

It hit him. The body left behind in the empty building was a work of art. A sculpture. The Polaroids had been taken to show the victim its very creation.

Inside his cell countless voices still told Nigal Adtombwe what he had to do. He tried to reassemble the past. At Sheffield city police station thirty-two years ago he had told them everything. The taller of the two detectives demanded to know why three weeks had elapsed since Jeremy Rose had decided to hang himself. He saw his friend hanging from the moon and could not say. He did not know how to, once it became clear they were not interested enough to believe him. They loosened their ties and rolled up their sleeves. They smelled of stale beer and cigarettes. He refused to leave their station. It was safe here: he was scared stiff. Too scared to go back, which was why he had come to them in the first place. He had tried to explain, three weeks too late.

They did not listen. The wall clock ticked. Time did not listen. To end it all the police let him make a statement. A full and complete three-page statement, which they took down, ready for him to sign. As long as you go back, they ordered. You must, you have to. Don't worry, all you have to do is go back and wait. Finally he agreed with their wall clock. He signed his name at the foot of the last page and went back. But for all the time Nigal Adtombwe had waited thirty-two years ago, neither of the two detectives ever returned.

The past still shouted, swore, screamed and whispered in his ears. He dared not mutter back. The monster he had murdered still lived, breathed and spoke inside his own skull. He could not kill it there. He tried to keep hold of the Polaroids. He wanted everything else to go away.

That morning they still asked Nigal Adtombwe why he had committed the murder. He told them. In between mumbles and silences he tried to rid himself of the past. It was a confession.

DC Wilet and DI Tilt listened. In between cassette tapes they listened to the voices inside the head of Nigal Adtombwe. No one had listened before.

'I saw him on television.'

Seventeen

Shift after shift Tilt and Wilet played back the tape recorder, attempting to decipher a morass of jumbled up words, sounds, mumbles and silence.

PAUSE. Glasses. *PAUSE. Indecipherable passage. PAUSE.* He. *Indecipherable passage.* He wore glasses. He never wore glasses. *PAUSE.* He wore glasses. *PAUSE.* To look at me. I knew it was him.

Even after they had transcribed the tapes and decoded its many tangled mutterings and manic flights, it hardly made sense. It never did – whatever Nigal Adtombwe told them. No one had listened to him before. It was like trying to scissor and paste together blood.

He was to tell them everything. Detective Inspector Tilt repeated his questions. 'Who wore these glasses?' he asked again. 'When did you see him on TV? What was his name?'

Their prisoner ignored their presence. His mouth stayed open, trapped. Eyes screwed shut, he remained in another world. To them he looked like a gargoyle high up on a cathedral roofline, a mask fixed there for centuries but carved from pain. Their tape recorder waited.

Peter Congreave was already waiting when Nigal Adtombwe first came to the city. Thirty-three years ago waiting on a platform between steam trains in 1965. The

154

prep school headmaster had wanted to shake hands with an eleven-year-old from Nigeria. The boy would not let go of his suitcase to leave his family with strangers. Their breaths tangled together above his head, lost admidst the height of adults and the steam of trains. The boy's family were already dead.

Suddenly the gargoyle cracked into countless sounds. Rushing to escape. To survive.

'A voice grows big inside me. Too big to hold. Push your fist through the tele. Smash his glasses. Quick – before it's too late. It's too late. I close my eyes, the voices swallow the room. It's him, the voices scream, controlling my brain. Stop him, stop him from talking to me. I can't. Voices don't change. He crawls outside my head and watches us all. Destroy him. Smash his face, I can't take this any more. Please destroy me.'

The two police officers watched a little saliva dribble from the corner of Adtombwe's mouth. Wilet pushed across the box of cheap tissues. His lips trembled between mouthings and lopsided words. Tilt raised a hand, as the act of a professional in control. Slow down, he was about to say. Take things slowly, one at a time. No need to rush; listen, sit still, stay calm. Adtombwe started to shake. Just his stare remained rigid, glazed eyes out of focus. The blank stare of a tiny creature, lost and alone. It pushed past time. They were witnessing someone hurtle towards madness.

They gave it a further full quarter of an hour. 'In shock,' the detective inspector wrote. 'Catatonic reaction? Hearing "voices" – psychosis?' After the interview they would need a psychiatrist.

Ruth Wilet's feet curled around her chair – they were still searching for a diagonal of lighter-coloured tiles that'd take her towards safety; her legs seemed to point in the opposite direction.

DI Tilt flicked through his notebook. He too needed a

way to make sense of this. He stopped at the circle he'd drawn in felt-tip when he saw the X-rays of the victim last January. Easter had come and gone, spring was here. The prisoner had been left in shock, alone, for nearly three months. John Tilt realized they had to wait for their prisoner to regain control of himself. Keep themselves pressed against him like a dressing next to a wound to staunch the flow of blood.

Time twisted around itself inside their tape-recorder cassettes, tighter and tighter. It seemed to unwind their prisoner's attempts to escape the past. Slowly his gargoyle face softened. Its mouth opened to sculpt the sound of words.

'It was an accident. I was never meant to see him. Not on TV. He had already hidden the remote. From the top of the set. It's not there. He told me to watch.

'How dare you appear on television, I tried to whisper. How dare you tell us how to educate our children after the things you've done? Not just to me, not just – No, he's still at it. I thought he'd died. Disappeared. Impossible. He's still at it, after all these years, hurting everyone. How dare we watch and let you get away with it? It doesn't stop. I yelled back at him – "How dare you!" But the programme had ended.'

It nearly made fragmentary sense to the two police officers. As much as the shattered remote control they had discovered crushed into Adtombwe's sitting-room carpet. What had happened to the TV?

'He let me rip out the plug. The screen still showed toes pointing down to the washroom floor. Each tile cold, they chilled my feet. The TV wouldn't switch off. He left behind his smell, of old creased paper, the smell of his aftershave.

'It had happened. It was real. My trousers stuck to me – I'd wet myself. I didn't know what to do. Except change my trousers. I keep spraying the room with air-freshener.'

Ruth Wilet wiped her eyes. She remembered how they had smarted when they'd entered the sitting room of his house. 'Can after can, every time he comes back.' Underneath the kitchen sink they had found dozens of empties.

'I try to sleep. Tried too hard. To forget. They've forced me to. Everyone else has, I c-c-c-can't. I ch-ch-ch-chuck the TV into the back of the van. Into the back of a river. One splash, and in the dark I see all the old valves flicker inside another set inside his room. Smell the dust and glue burning into each other.' Adtombwe drew breath. 'It's harder now. I'm too old to pretend to be inside a television set. I did once at the Cutlers'.' Their prisoner spoke directly to the detective inspector. 'You're staring at me.'

DI Tilt did not realize he had been. He glanced to DC Wilet; it was becoming vital the interview did not stall. The tapes recorded everything. Played back and transcribed, they'd become their map of Nigal Adtombwe's world. However mad it was, it held the truth to the Reddlewood case.

Adtombwe waited for Tilt to finish writing. 'It's on the tape,' their prisoner whispered. 'He's taken everything else. Friends, family, he's stolen them. With a few words, they're gone.

'Instead of people I see creatures. Birds, fish, animals from the furthest places you can imagine. From tomorrow. Bits and pieces, I create creatures from scrap. Instead of feelings, I've strange creatures made from things people throw away. You've seen them, haven't you?'

Nigal Adtombwe's eyes lit up for less than a second. The sculptures above the Hole in the Road, at Dagnell Crescent and blasting bay six seemed alive, ready to kill them all inside the interview room.

'He does the same, only with people. He takes them. Changes them, turns them into creatures. Into what he wants them to be, then he throws them away. Scrap. Not

157

just TVs. I've kept all his rubbish inside my head for years. I'm one of his creatures. Inside the dark I drive and drive until I find a church and pray. He sits next to me. Cruelty has a human heart, he whispers in my ear. God is Evil.'

Adtombwe stared at the space opposite, between the two police officers, as though waiting for them to draw up another, invisible chair. A fourth person had entered the room. The man he had murdered.

'I stop. The TV company gives me the name of the school where he's head teacher now. This wasn't a voice inside me. It's real. Where? Ripondale College, they repeated. North of Ilkley. I go there. It's just like the Cutlers', except larger. I turn round and go back, I couldn't meet him face to face. He knows I'm too small.'

Tilt held up his hand. 'Just a moment, Mr Adtombwe. The tape's nearly finished. Constable Wilet?'

'Interview suspended at 10.17 hours.' She held back a questioning glance towards Tilt. He looked dead to the world this morning. Nearly half the tape remained unrecorded. She leant over the table to remove both cassettes. He wrote brief notes on each of their boxes and opened a drawer on their side of the table. It was full of blank cassettes. 'Oh dear, empty. Ruth, could you?' She took the half-used cassettes.

One of Tilt's notes read: 'Wawner and Kirk to check name and status of Head of Ripondale College + contact Locality Mental Health Team.'

'Do you need the toilet, a glass of water, a drink of some kind, Mr Adtombwe?'

Mr Adtombwe shook his head at the empty space opposite. 'No. Don't leave. Stay,' he mouthed. 'They want me to talk to you, Mr Congreave.' The door closed. They waited till Ruth Wilet returned with extra cassettes.

The tapes whirred. The recording needles rose and fell. The interview room clock ticked.

158

'I write a letter. I tried to ring but the telephone smelled of his aftershave. He rang the day after I sent the letter. It mentioned the TV. He said we had to talk.

'The train was late. I needed to be early. It was different. I knew what to expect, he didn't. It was my turn to say what happened next. Strange, I could plan, for the first time. Not be pushed into it. I'd set things up, listened to the voices. They tell me to break into the empty factory, to work out what to do. We had changed, changed round I mean, haven't we? I was the master, he the boy; I have to decide. This time I'm in control – it's frightening.'

Their prisoner leant forward. 'Detective inspector, you're the only other person who's ever come to meet me.'

DI Tilt was puzzled. He couldn't think where or when.

'At the funeral. I thought you'd bury him. Put him away under ground so he'd never escape. Instead I feel his ashes fall onto my coat like the spit of a monster.'

Three months earlier Nigal Adtombwe had watched the empty rails, ready to meet his teacher's train. The station had hardly altered, yet the train still came in as a surprise. He held out his arm to shake hands with people who were dead. He spoke to them as his eyes scanned the carriage doors. The train stopped, the carriage doors opened one by one. Peter Congreave was the last to leave the first class section. He waited on the carriage step, peering up and down the platform as the eleven-year-old Nigal had. Each was looking for someone he did not know. Someone else rushed past. Nigal thought it looked like Jez as a young man. It wasn't. Congreave didn't seem to notice, just removed his glasses. To release the smell of the aftershave that preceded the touch of his skin. On the platform it tangled with their breaths above their heads.

'There you are, Nigal. I almost didn't recognize you. No longer a lower school boy, but a man. Quite splendid – it looks like snow.'

Nigal Adtombwe did not reply. A guard tried to squeeze behind them to slam the carriage doors shut. Congreave took a step forward, Adtombwe a step back. Neither dared breathe an extra word until the train left. Just for a second they were both small boys.

'It's cold,' Mr Congreave said. It was. 'What were you thinking of? A drink somewhere? We can hardly stand here all night, can we?'

Adtombwe used to hate those rhetorical questions. They hid the truth.

'Please excuse my manners, Mr Congreave. Would you like to visit my studio? See how it works.'

'That'd be interesting, yes, something of a privilege.' They crossed the road and walked towards the car park. 'It surprised me to see the piece in the *Evening Post* last year. I always had you down as a lawyer, something official. You were so organized and diligent in your work. Still, a credit to the Cutlers' – and yourself, of course. Do you go back often? Not at all?'

Congreave watched Adtombwe shake his head.

'A pity. The boys would gain so much from hearing about your experiences.'

'I lecture at the university – sculpture fails to pay.'

'No family?' his old headmaster asked when they reached his van.

'No. I live on my own.'

'We've four. The youngest's still at the Cutlers'. And three grandchildren. There's never a moment's peace. However grown up they seem, they're still your children. I envy you, Adtombwe.'

Nigal didn't need reminding his own family were all dead. They both knew that.

'But I wouldn't change a thing, Nigal. Not a thing, you understand. Not a single thing.'

'There's a lever under the seat if you need more legroom.'

The van stopped in the middle of the road. Its driver had missed the turning for Carrdyke Lane.

'How long have you had this studio of yours?' Congreave asked.

'Not long,' Adtombwe replied while he tried to find reverse gear. He was ready to rent an empty section of the building to construct a piece from bridge girders when Reddlewoods had closed down. He tried to wipe the clamminess from his hands. The gears still slipped as he turned the van.

'Do you know, Nigal, in all the years we lived near Sheffield we never visited this part? Nasty destitute factories. Hardly the place for you.'

It hit Nigal Adtombwe. Nearly winded him, like a blow to the stomach. Mr Congreave had done this before. Met his victims. Years, decades later. Many times before. To stay in control, all the time.

'Why not?' Adtombwe replied. A rhetorical question of his own. He was learning. This time he couldn't let him get away with it. The brakes slewed them to a stop. 'A boys' boarding school is hardly the place for a pederast, wouldn't you say?'

Adtombwe repeated the question. More slowly, until the other man had to listen. There was no answer.

In the interview room Nigal Adtombwe turned to the two police officers. 'I should've walked away. He looked down and it was too late.' They waited for him to continue. 'I think I killed him.'

'Yes. We think you did,' Tilt confirmed. Their prisoner now seemed calmer, more aware of his situation. Perhaps they were gaining his confidence. 'Tell us what happened next. In the yard.'

'I told him to get out. He'd kept fucking the insides of our skulls long after he'd finished fucking the arse out of our trousers. I didn't want him near me. He didn't move.'

Neither did DI Funeral nor DC Lady. Motive, a hungry force, prowled round the room. Until satisfied, it had screamed and roared into the ears of the possessed, where it killed all other reason or madness to impel the act into reality. This was how Nigal Adtombwe had murdered Peter Congreave. Then it escaped and evaded capture as best it could: a hurt, hurtful beast, after release it feeds just upon itself. They saw how Adtombwe would only tell them the truth. He had lost control of events years ago. Lost control of the pain and the misery, as they kept hold of his despair.

Nigal Adtombwe switched off the engine. He and Peter Congreave each listened to the silence. An old clock had stopped ticking.

'Get out!' he yelled inside the van.

'Please, Nigal. You're upset. I know you're upset. Allow me to explain, won't you?'

The driver's side door opened.

'Listen, Nigal. It doesn't have to be like this, believe me. Let me help, let me help you. Why won't you let me help?'

The interior light caught the passenger's eyes. The van's driver readied himself to run away.

'Nigal, I understand. Call me Peter.'

Peter Congreave watched Adtombwe turn very slowly back round towards him.

'That's what you said when Jez died – "Call me Peter" . . . Out of the fucking car. Now!'

He saw the steering lock in Adtombwe's hand. He undid the seatbelt to leap out. Adtombwe found a torch and crowbar in the back. Congreave twisted away from his side of the car. He thought he was about to be beaten to death. Struggling to his feet, he slipped on the icy cobbles, banged the side of his head just above the right eye. He felt for the bruise while Adtombwe pulled him up by the sleeve of his coat. Neither dared to run away. The crowbar levered open

162

the padlock hasp and the torch found the power switches. 'Stay here. Sorry, I've forgotten the rope.'

They walked through the office and stepped onto the gantry. Peter Congreave looked at the dirty machinery in the same way he stared at a class of pupils. He didn't need machinery to control people. He bent people's minds as a smith with a hard heavy hammer bends soft steel. Metal to metal. Welded them to shapes of his own design and choosing. He used his hands and head to mould flesh. He needed people to work with.

Nigal Adtombwe had to bring him here. The machinery seemed to cut out his power. The two-faced charm that hid his grimy appetite was a tool, sharp and cunning, but useless without pliant raw material to work on. Charisma now became his weakness: he could hardly be evil without possessing the will of others. Adtombwe had found a way in. Here was only machinery: dead machinery.

Congreave did not know what to do. Neither did Nigal Adtombwe.

'Where are the sculptures?'

'You'll see,' answered Adtombwe, but Peter Congreave had already guessed. There were no sculptures. At least, nothing completed.

'Remember Jez, Mr Congreave?'

'Jez?' It only sounded like a question; Congreave had replied too quickly, he knew who Adtombwe meant.

'Yes; Jez. Jez Rose. Sit down. Sit down!'

Congreave glanced back at the gantry steps but walked to an old office chair in a corner of the bay.

'No! In the middle, on the turntable, where we can see you.' This was his favourite method to humiliate a boy in public. It was different in private. 'Take the chair, sit down and tell the class exactly what you did to put yourself in this position. And why – Peter.'

His eyes protested but his body obeyed. It had to. After

163

thirty years their relative strength was reversed: Adtombwe now towered over him.

'I did it all to help you, Nigal. Everything.'

'Jez Rose hanged himself. Did you say the same to him too?'

Nigal Adtombwe ignored the two police officers, and the two cassettes inside their tape recorder. He was talking to the fourth person in the room. The man he was about to murder.

Peter Congreave had expected just more fawning adoration, not this; he had been a fool to come. He tried to explain: 'Jeremy Rose's death was unfortunate.'

'Shut up! Who asked you to speak? Shut your mouth, and keep it shut.'

Congreave watched Adtombwe closely, ready for the moment this mad black man's back turned. Best not to make eye contact. Head dropped, he had to follow the maniac's footsteps through spent abrasive towards his chair. A finger jerked up his chin. Hurt angry eyes burnt into his own.

'You're not listening. Don't try to escape. It's too late – for both of us. Just listen. I walk down the corridor from the dorm to the washroom. You didn't know that, did you? It's dark, but my eyes climb up his body. It doesn't move, not by itself. It swings from a dressing-gown cord. The dressing gown hangs open. Hands dangle from its sleeves like gloves on a string inside a raincoat, to stop you losing them. My hands reach out, they touch his legs. Cold, cold. My fingers are wet. Jez has soiled himself through his pyjamas. I stretch up on tiptoe, to reach as far as I can. His toes point to a pool of urine and faeces that run around an upturned bucket. I hold him tight and try to stop his body swinging from the moon. I stub my foot. He didn't kill himself. You did.'

Peter Congreave chose his words carefully. He always

did. The tape recorder recorded two people inside one voice. 'Jeremy's death was unfortunate, Nigal. There was nothing you or I could do about it. Not then, and certainly not now. He was a troubled boy. We both know that.'

Adtombwe tried not to listen. Congreave looked so calm in his chair. So assured and gentle. Once people knew him well enough to trust him, he had a way of telling lies so that even when you knew he was fibbing, you wanted to believe he had told you the truth. The whole truth and nothing but the truth. Like a gift, something special. Something you had to take. It was magic; the truths that hurt seemed to vanish into thin air. He was too charming for words. Nigal Adtombwe very nearly gave in to his old teacher. He had needed to believe him, and he did, especially the lies. Because then the truth, the real truth, couldn't matter.

'We did our level best to help poor Jeremy. We all did.'

The voices inside Adtombwe's head told Congreave and Jez to shut up.

'Did we? Is that why you buggered the shit out of him?'

Congreave's jaw dropped. It was a surprise to both of them. The boys' headmaster had never realized that Jez had told Nigal everything. He had Jeremy Rose down as just another weak boy, ready prey. Who'd wanted to hang himself rather than tell others of their secret world.

Secret no more. For a moment Congreave showed his fear. The shock hurtled by as fast as it had come, a drill breaking through a piece of metal; a gap between dark and less dark tiles. His eyes flashed cunning, hatred and cruelty. Astronomers glimpse something similar within a black hole: the origins of malevolence, a shred of emptiness that betrays the entire universe with the speed of light. Every speck of it, every hidden corner of existence, every sin, every deceit. His secrets were evil, and his evil secret. They could never disappear.

Nigal Adtombwe started to realize how Peter Congreave controlled them all. It made him change his mind. 'You thought I didn't know. After all these years, Mr Congreave, you thought I did not know. Jez caught me mumbling to myself, to my family. It was easier than writing a letter without reply. They spoke to me, muttering nonsense. That's how we became friends. You thought he was too weak to tell anyone what you did to him, but Jez understood what it's like to be left out on your own. It was happening to him. He told me everything. Every instance of sodomy, every time your dick went up his arse. He was so in love with you.'

'It wasn't like that.'

'Come on, don't tell me you didn't know. The whole junior school had you worked out. Sneaking a peek in the showers, through the doorless lavatory cubicles –'

'That's ridiculous, Nigal.'

'Dead right, you teachers were almost a joke to us. Bottleneck Somerville, Cocksure Congreave. Almost, but not quite, because you had the power. Except for Jez. He was different. He worshipped you, cared for you, and in the end loved you enough to die for you. True Romance stuff. You weren't that vain never to see it. Stuffing your prick up his twelve-year-old arse broke his heart. A proper advertisement for pederasty.'

Congreave didn't look too surprised. 'I'm sorry. I didn't realize.'

'I'll bet.'

'If you did, you'd lose. Before you tell me to be quiet, I'll explain. You don't understand, Nigal. I still remember you and Rose were marvellously good friends. It pleased us staff. His parents were posted overseas with the RAF, and yours were lost during the Biafran War. There were many friendships like that at the Cutlers'. Rose was small for his age, but he helped educate you. He was older, he knew this

166

country, he helped you learn to adapt, become part of how we behave here. He only told you the things he thought you needed to know. How on earth could you have found out that what he told you simply wasn't true?'

Tears tried to weep through Adtombwe's eyelashes; he wanted Congreave to be straight, to tell him the truth.

His old headmaster watched a finger touch a cut-out square of flesh on his cheek where tears should have run. Some primitive tribal markings or the like. He did not see the pain, pain that Adtombwe wanted to cut away with something like an angle grinder. He was judging the time to make good his escape.

Adtombwe kept walking round the chair. In 1965 Peter Congreave had taken him from the railway station to the Cutlers' School. He had been trying to escape ever since. 'You promised me you'd help. You hugged me, you held me. "Pretend it's never happened," you said. "It'll go away." I've tried but his body still hangs down from the moon, its reflection in his urine. How could I tell you that? It gets worse. The way Jez mentioned how you first touched him. Almost accidentally, your thigh thrust into his bottom as we crowded into the refectory. "Don't push," you ordered as you pushed. He told me how he'd pushed his bottom back into your thigh. You didn't resist or pull away. He told me how he felt at that moment. The wonder and joy, at how his hero had responded. His God. There's more, there's always more. What did you study in your rooms? He was your project; he didn't make it up. Tell me, you're still here. How do you kill the past? It's coming back to you, isn't it? It should do, you planned it.'

Congreave's lips tightened together. Adtombwe would never understand. Just like Rose before him. There were too many boys who did not understand. Not even the needs of their own bodies. There was no point in attempting to explain. They'd never listen.

167

'You don't understand, do you?' demanded Adtombwe.

Congreave kept silent.

'Jez was heartbroken that Easter. We went to his aunt's and uncle's. It was wonderful – the first time I'd seen television, the first time I was known just by my first name. Three weeks' life imprisonment for him. All Jez could talk about was you. Only his body was there. His spirit remained somewhere in the sky, up with the astronauts circling the earth. Down here he forced me to rush everything, even brushing my teeth. "No time to gargle, Tombie," he'd say. "We must get back closer to him sooner than soon, quicker than quick. I have to see him. Just have to." You were his Gemini and Apollo, Mr Congreave. Remember the first night back?'

Their old headmaster showed no sign of remembering. Or forgetting. It was best to do neither. He showed no emotion at all.

'The dorms were always quiet. Jez was the last to undress. "I didn't think it would be like that," he whispered to me after lights out. I crept across the wooden floor. "Peter promised me it would be wonderful, and in a way it was, but he didn't tell me how it would hurt." Jez described in meticulous, loving detail how you buggered the arse out of him. He had to skive off games, the bruises spread right across his backside. "It hurt so much, Tombie. Is that why it can be so wonderful?" You tell me, Mr Congreave. You ought to know. You did it.'

Congreave shook his head. Faced with the truth there was nothing much else he could do. Nothing he dared admit. He decided to allow Adtombwe to continue. There was no proof.

'He let my fingers touch his tears. I didn't want to go near. You already had, you'd taken him away from me. Don't ask me to believe he'd made it up, he told me everything. Everything you did. The bruises, the pain, the fist-fucking. You never cared, did you?' Adtombwe looked him straight in the eye. 'You don't know how to.'

His prisoner stared straight back. 'How dare you say that, Nigal? What's got into you?'

'Don't pretend, Mr Congreave. He wanted to sleep with me – that made you start. You're jealous. Don't shake your head, I know you are. Over the summer Jez changed. He tried to turn our fights and wrestles into a squeeze and hug, a little more, bit by bit, each day of our holidays. His hands working their way underneath our clothes to get to my skin. To try to do to me what you did to him. He started to become like you. Broader, stronger, heavier. In a matter of weeks he'd grown taller than me to match the drop in his voice. He showed me how he could make his penis grow big – nearly as big as yours, he bragged. "Hold it still," he said. I watched. "Here, let me show you with yours," he said. I wouldn't. I wanted to but I couldn't let him try.'

Nigal Adtombwe stared at his hands. 'I didn't want anybody to touch me. Not even Jez.'

Peter Congreave started to rise from his chair. His captor pushed him back down. The elder man's hands cupped themselves around his own groin. Not through fear, or arousal, but simple greed. He wanted more. More of those young boys.

In the interview room their prisoner sounded almost sane – except that he was speaking to a man who had ceased to exist. The man he had sandblasted to death. Tilt and Wilet only had to listen.

Inside the blasting bay Peter Congreave waited for Nigal Adtombwe to finish his tirade. He started to clock-watch, he didn't want to miss the last train. He didn't want to spend a moment longer in this dreadful place.

Adtombwe slowed down. 'It was over for Jez, only he

169

didn't know it. After those summer holidays Jez came back to school in love with you. Lust, worship and devotion, in every way an adolescent can imagine. He was no longer a boy, a little boy. He wanted to share with you his ideas and dreams, his plans and ambitions, his life and his body. He didn't want you to play with him. He wanted something real. Not much, a drop of love, some affection. A little of what he had given you. You'd finished with him, though. You didn't want him, but you couldn't be bothered to mention it.

'Don't look away. He needed you, Congreave. Each time you rejected him, each time you ignored his longings, those tiny seedlings of desire you had propagated that spring, they grew and grew until they burst out of his head – you must've seen it. An overgrown jungle of longing where he was now lost, inside a crazed passion you had begun. All Jez could do was talk to me. About how you cared for him, how you understood his tiniest thought. He'd sworn me to secrecy. About how you made his life complete, worth living. Don't turn away.

'You couldn't share his dream worlds. You hadn't created them. You just filled his arse and head with your balls. That's your secret. You couldn't cope with boys once they started to turn into men. Once their voices and testicles dropped, you lost all interest. You didn't even want to screw them. You fucked him and dumped him. You refused to handle a thirteen-year-old's emotions because you only wanted to screw twelve-year-old arseholes.'

For the first time Nigal Adtombwe looked angry. Congreave appeared not to notice.

'Jez had no one else to go to. I tried to understand but I'd no idea what he was talking about. My penis wouldn't grow large however hard we managed to rub. His whole relationship with you, not just the sex, was mad, bad, an insane forest, but Jez would have none of it. This time he

170

was lying, deluding himself. He said I was jealous of you two. I had been, but there was no more "you two". You saw to that. I tried to tell Jez because I loved him. That's why I'd been envious. I wanted to love him. I still do.'

This really was ridiculous, Congreave thought. He suppressed the urge to laugh out loud.

'Inside the jungle he waited for signals, and if the wait became too long he imagined them instead. The fewer signs you gave, the deeper he went into the jungle to find them. He made me swear to tell no one, especially not you. He confided in me to back up these delusions, and with each delusion he went further than the last. What was I meant to do?'

Adtombwe stopped between shadows. 'I was twelve. I had last seen my family travel back across the Benue into a jungle forest. I thought you'd notice. Talk to him, bring his agony to an end. It went on for day after day, week after week. It seemed endless. I tried my best. And what did you do? Abandoned him, as you leched after the next juicy little prepubescent boy.'

Quite ridiculous. Congreave watched Adtombwe's shoes, laced up the right way. He dared not look him in the eye. Not yet.

Adtombwe had stopped. He listened to the sounds that defined the night Jez died. Footsteps. Everything he had heard, touched. His feet kicked at the spent abrasive dust.

'He couldn't keep you once you'd thrown him away. At last he knew. He must've caught you at it, halfway up the next arse of the month. I bet he spoke to you, appealed to you; but of course he no longer appealed to you. That night he said nothing to me. No dreams, no delusions, no secret messages hidden from all but you and him. Nothing. I thought you'd spoken to him, and Jez, my friend Jez, the old Jez Rose would return. I've thought about it a lot. You did speak to him, didn't you? That night. His feet crept across the wood of the dormitory floor into the dark corridor of jungle to meet you one more time. He was my only friend and I thought he could love me. He never came back.'

Peter Congreave glanced at his watch. It seemed to have stopped. He'd probably missed the last train, not that it really mattered.

'You've admitted it yourself, Nigal. He was deluded. It's all nonsense.'

'You couldn't care less. You couldn't wait to get your disgusting hands on the next small boy that came your way, and the next, to persuade them to take your prick up their sweet little arses. One after the other seduced, for years on end. Being such prepubescent darlings they couldn't get it up to screw you back. You were frightened of them, weren't you? Shit scared. What was it you said so eloquently on television: "We are all responsible for the whole child." You weren't interested in the whole child, only the holes in our backsides. Jeremy Rose was one more defenceless fuck to you, Peter Pederast Congreave. Just another fuck to devour. We were children, not just your fucking victims. Children!'

Congreave had dusted the seat with his handkerchief, pulled the creases of his trousers straight, to sit through all his former pupil had to say. Adtombwe had expected him to resist. But it was clear he did not need to resist, or deny. Simply ignore the pain he had inflicted upon others, as he had done for decades. There was no sense of concern or feeling; these children could have been succulent fruit from a grove in a private orchard. To Congreave it was what they were, but Adtombwe had never realized this till now.

'Take off your clothes.'

Congreave misunderstood the rope in Adtombwe's hands. 'No, I'm not interested in men, or bondage, Nigal –

I thought you knew that. And I'm no paedophile. I love children, the whole child. Rose took his own life, I didn't. I love children.'

'You mean he'd've killed himself if you hadn't fucked him brainless and dumped him. He was thirteen years old. Take your clothes off or I'll kill you.'

'Hell hath no fury greater than two schoolboys scorned.'

Nigal Adtombwe's fist went to smash the side of his former headmaster's face with all the years of suffering left in his body. It stopped a fraction away from the bruise around the eye caused by the slip on the cobbles. 'I'm sorry. Get up.'

Congreave's eyes didn't move away from the fist. His bowels had started to loosen; he was scared shitless. No one with such physical power had threatened him before. No one he had controlled had ever fought back. Without another word he started to remove his clothes. His body lay creased around its joints where the skin had started to lose its shape. Adtombwe almost laughed at its folds and goosebumps, they looked so ridiculous. It was cold. As cold as the body of a boy hanging from the moonlight through a washroom window. Neither of them was much like Apollo.

Naked, Congreave watched Adtombwe wipe his hands very slowly into his clothes until his sweat mingled with their smell and the oily stench of the workshop, to block out the fragrance of his own aftershave. He felt the blood around his own eye. He thought Adtombwe was about to bugger him. He had never been buggered before. The thought had never crossed his mind. It scared yet thrilled him. He let himself be tied up. The knots weren't too tight or too loose. They both closed their eyes. Nigal Adtombwe wanted him to escape. To leave him in peace. Their lives apart were over.

*

Ruth Wilet found herself inside blasting bay six. She overheard two men's voices between the machinery. She tried not to listen but failed. Tilt placed a hand over hers. She pushed it away. She didn't want to be near a man. In the police force as well as the Cutlers' School they abused everybody. In the interview room the three of them listened to the past. She tried to pretend the cassette tapes weren't going round, that none of it had ever happened.

Cold, Congreave tried not to shiver, tried to explain without pleading. 'We were friends, Nigal.'

Adtombwe took a step back. It felt cruel to watch his old headmaster's goosebumps struggle against the rope. Cruel and painful. He wanted their abuser to know exactly how it had felt every day of the thirty-two years since he had discovered the body of Jeremy Rose.

Congreave was worried that Adtombwe would leave without giving him a chance to explain, persuade and then win him back. He was jealous of the two boys' friendship, he admitted to himself, and it drove him to continue. 'I wanted to give you something of what you had with Jeremy. Remember how we watched television together?'

'I remember the camera' – the pictures their headmaster took of them watching black and white television, black and white humping in front of Panorama, the whirr of a sixteen-millimetre home movie camera on a tripod, recording bare posteriors for posterity. They were exhibits in a private museum. Adtombwe had spoken more to himself than to Congreave. It was the dead he addressed next: 'I'm sorry, Jez, I never really believed you until it . . . ha-ha-ha-ha-happ – He did it to me too.'

'That's hardly fair,' interrupted Congreave. Lust was to be his final defence. 'Remember it was you who came to me. I never forced you to do anything. Not then, and certainly not now. I treated you in exactly the same way as Jeremy. I let you sleep with me for comfort's sake, to share our mutual loss. I pitied you. But I remember your body. Not because it was black. That was unusual but not necessarily memorable. It was its . . . its malleability. Yes, its compliant malleability.' Congreave's lips lingered around the phrase, licking its nuance into life. 'It didn't seem too tender or tight, closed or inviting, weak or strong. You were strange – perhaps like your sculptures. Quite different from all the other boys I've slept with, and there have been many; dozens of them, at least. It wouldn't do to keep count, I'd have to remember their names. I remembered yours.'

He licked his mouth. 'I'm a caring man. It's important I don't harm the boys I sleep with. To a greater or lesser extent they all enjoyed it, invited it, gave little signals only for me to see. See for yourself, if you like, on film or video. Why else do men who slept with me as boys now let me sleep with their sons? In a way, through public school, they pay me to do it. But you were different. The possibility of pleasure was denied your body, which only redoubled the sensation in mine. Wickedly dangerous, I admit, but if the truth be told I nearly wanted you beyond puberty, to possess your innocent obedience for ever.' Congreave paused, then smiled. 'And in a way I do. You were better than Jez. Much better. If you say I killed him, it was only to get close to your dark, malleable body. A desire beyond dreams.'

Nigal heard the whirr of the home movie camera again: it was all too real. Peter Congreave seemed unaware of his erection, naked, rubbing against the ropes which bound him to the chair – and Nigal Adtombwe.

'It was as though you didn't know who you were.'

Tears at last fell down his captor's cheeks. 'I still don't,' Adtombwe heard himself say. 'Of course they never protest. We had to do what you said. How could I get Jez back? Inside your camera you let me watch your cock

175

grow hard. Bigger, stronger than Jez's. Let me hold it. Kiss and lick it. Take it in my mouth while your fist fucked my arse. Hang onto it, let its magic soothe its pain. I thought if I let you fuck me I could become Jez or he'd return to us. Reverse time – let him live again. I was twelve. How dare I be different? Only I knew you'd abandon me. I knew, and I let it happen. However evil you were, you still seemed to love us. That's what you murdered. Love. Every time you fucked us. Even its idea. "The only thing necessary, in life as in art, is to tell the truth." Ugliness is reality. We're ugly. Jez must've come to you that night and told you he'd kill himself. You did nothing. Nothing. He told you he'd kill himself and you did nothing except stick your fucking penis in me. The perfect short-trousered fuck. Shall I suck it off for you now?'

Congreave looked down. Adtombwe knew too much, far too much. The erection had vanished, his limp dick a machine past its task.

Nigal turned to leave. Then he realized what had happened at the far end of the dormitory corridor.

In the interview room the two police officers expected their suspect to continue.

'If he'd not spoken I'd have left him there. To escape or die, it doesn't matter. He'd heard me tell the truth – I'm sorry, I can't forget.'

Nigal Adtombwe leant forward and rested his head in his hands. There was more to be said, to be exhumed then buried again. They had been listening for a long time but he did not know if it had altered anything.

'Do you want to take a break?' DI Tilt asked after three minutes of silence. 'A glass of water?'

Adtombwe's head nodded. Tilt indicated to Wilet to halt the tape recorder. The record button clicked, the sound level needles went dead.

176

'This isn't the first time I've tried to explain what happened, d-d-d-detective inspector. Don't let Peter Congreave inside your head, it's far worse than his fist up your arse.'

Tilt was ready to leave the room. The reason Adtombwe gave for attending Congreave's funeral remained wedged against his consciousness: 'I had to make sure he was dead.'

At the door Tilt could see Adtombwe was still trying.

Eighteen

As the second tape ended, their prisoner had asked to use the toilet. DC Wilet was waiting outside the washroom door, listening for a cistern flush. She heard footsteps hurry towards her from opposite ends of the corridor. The officers hardly slowed as they caught sight of each other. She waited for them to collide.

Tilt was on his way back from an empty section office. Now he realized where DS Wawner and DC Kirk had been called away to: they followed just behind Jack Singleterry. DCI Naylor was hurrying to keep up with them.

Wilet stepped back and stood next to the door to the washroom. Nowhere inside the police station seemed safe to her any more.

Detective Superintendent Singleterry stamped himself into DI Tilt's face. 'What the fuck's happening here, inspector? Didn't I tell you to search all the missing person files, not just South Yorkshire?'

'No, sir. You did not.'

The reverse was true: Singleterry had buried Tilt's recommendation to extend the search into the region as a whole.

Singleterry's anger poured past Tilt's denial. 'I've just had it from that bitch from the Serious Crime Squad, DCS Birtels. She's trying to boil your balls in vinegar. Don't come the innocent with me, Tilt, or I'll fucking stiff you for sticking your hands in your fucking church's till, so help me God.'

They all knew Jack Singleterry had never wanted to see this case solved. It had hurt him, so he'd hurt anyone who happened to stand in his way, especially DI prickface, holier-than-thou, shit-wouldn't-melt-in-his-mouth Tilt. The perfect sacrifice: he hated the bastard. Sergeant Wawner totted up the swear words carefully. The canteen had a sweep running on the final total.

'Your victim's been on their missing persons list for months – and now that black bitch Birtels knows it's your fault. You've gone too far this time, Tilt. Far too fucking far.'

'Sir,' Tilt managed to squeeze past the hail of invective.

Behind Singleterry, DCI Naylor looked at his shoes. He had watched Jack knock countless suspects off balance just with words, then knock them down and give them a good kicking into the bargain. Tilt was just a policeman. The other men inched back down the corridor. They had never seen Mad Jack this mad before. It frightened them.

Tilt and Wilet stood their ground. They had nowhere else to go.

Ruth Wilet and Bill Naylor half-exchanged a glance. She tried not to cry, be a girlie. She remembered the pantomime horse image, Naylor's head propped halfway up Singleterry's backside. It helped. She had made up her mind. This section destroyed its own. She did not want to spend her life in a police force that spilled corrosive emotions onto corroded emotions. Everyone ended up damaged. Too damaged to leave.

'The prisoner needs help,' was all her inspector said.

'Does he bollocks. You read him his rights. He refused a brief.'

'Not a lawyer,' Tilt shouted back. 'A nurse. Someone to talk to, to listen, just listen – psychiatric help.'

'Fuck me. Why the shit am I bothering to listen to this crap?'

Their eyes met. Everything inside Singleterry hated Tilt, and now Tilt hated Singleterry back every bit as much. Neither would give way. The others watched from a distance.

It had been safer inside the interview room. John Tilt kept hold of the door handle; Ruth Wilet stood with her back to the wall opposite. Out here the truth was meaningless. Only its danger survived.

Tilt tried his hardest to keep quiet. It was his word against his superior's. He had no way out, not on his own.

'You're fucking lost for words, you spineless piece of shit. I've had it up to here protecting the likes of you from that slag-faced tart Birtels. Not when you've been canoodling with little Miss Wilet here to stick in a written grievance.'

'Sorry?'

'Don't look so surprised, little Inspector Perfect. We all know now.'

John Tilt did not know.

Ruth Wilet had kept her confidential letter to the assistant chief constable secret. The assistant chief constable hadn't. It was serious stuff. Not just a complete lack of support on relief from February, stuck in a derelict factory which stank of piss because policemen had stood in a corner and let loose a skinful. She could have been shot or blown up with DCI Naylor at Airport Van Hire, because she'd been forced into using her partner's private car. Her immediate superiors, Tilt included, had done nothing to support her. The assistant chief constable decided to have a quiet word, man to man, with Jack Singleterry: 'Lesbian, sir; she and DI Tilt are a pair of bad apples. Leave it with me.'

'Inadequate back up,' Singleterry summarized now. 'Or was she really complaining about your personal one-to-one performance not giving her complete satisfaction? Didn't you know she's a lez?'

He didn't need to know, or guess. Singleterry and Tilt stood toe to toe.

'There is very little that you can do about it now, loverboy. You should've kept your little girlie quiet. She's sure to lose both her lovely long legs right up to her plonkbox.'

Tilt drew back a fist. Singleterry smiled. This was the reaction he wanted: to kill the truth, to bury its dangers.

'God, you're a totally inadequate turd. Why are you a policeman?'

John Tilt had no answer. Neither did Bill Naylor, or Graeme Wawner, or Richard Kirk.

'Fuck you, sir.' They all turned to Detective Constable Wilet. She tried not to blush, tried not to cry. It had been a hard letter to write. She wished she had never written it. 'You're an evil piece of shit. That's why you're a copper.'

Within a stunned silence they turned as one to their detective superintendent. Jack Singleterry did not know what to say except yes. He went to smash the living daylights out of Ruth Wilet.

DCI Naylor moved in between them. He was tired of having to rescue Jack Singleterry from himself. His face was blotched and unshaven, his shirt collar as grimy as his breath with drink and unwashed skin. His stomach hurt all the time, his eyes were red raw.

Ruth Wilet moved out of range. She had never appreciated how tall Bill Naylor was when he stood up straight.

'Right, Jack,' he commanded, hand pushing into the small of Singleterry's shoulders. 'We need to talk, now! And you lot, if you know what's good for you, get back to work.'

Before they left, Naylor handed to Tilt a one-page fax

181

taken from their section intray. 'Here you are, John. Read this.' It was the only time their DCI had ever called DI Tilt by his Christian name. At last Bill Naylor seemed to have remembered where he had met Nigal Adtombwe before. 'Fuck you, Jack Singleterry,' he said, not caring who heard.

Fuck me, Sergeant Wawner said to himself. Thirty-seven profanities. He had swept the pool.

SERIOUS CRIME SQUAD   Leeds
                        tel: 0113 536 4793
                        fax: 0113 536 4770
                        e-mail: scs@wtykpl.ho.gov.uk

FAX   1 of 1

To: DC Kirk, City Section, Sheffield

From: DS Carr-Roberts

Re: Headteacher of Ripondale College, nr Studley, North Yorkshire.

Peter Congreave reported missing by his wife Monday 27 January.

No evidence of whereabouts to date.

Enquiries have located major paedophile and child-pornography ring, related to international juvenile prostitution networks, including the world wide web, but details of positive links to Congreave or his disappearance not yet totally established.

Investigations currently involve both SCS and Scotland Yard Vice Squad operations.

Imperative DSupt. Singleterry contacts DCS Birtels at once.

End of fax.

Nineteen

In a total of seventy years' shared service Bill Naylor had never answered back.

Jack Singleterry waited till the DCI had closed the door behind them. Then he told him the truth. 'I don't care if you drink on duty, Billy Boy, but you're pissed out of your fucking skull. You smell like shit and look worse.'

Naylor didn't reply straight away. He wasn't quite pissed enough to. Of course he'd drunk far more than usual, ever since they had arrested Nigal Adtombwe. At home a handwritten letter from Mrs Eccles lay next to his kitchen sink.

Sorry, Mr Naylor, but especially the state of the bathroom and the bed linen is too much.
I am sorry, really, I am. I know it's not my place, but perhaps you ought to see a doctor or someone.

Bill Naylor already had. He had failed his routine medical. The medics told him what he really already knew. All the abdominal pain was his liver, pancreas and endocrine system drowning in alcohol. He had nodded his head but he'd gone past caring about his body packing up. Next to Mrs Eccles's letter were three piles of ten pound notes, wages for each week since she'd left. They failed to bring her back. Bill Naylor did not think they would, but he didn't have her home address to send them on to. Who cared? His dad had to die going down a pit. He had to die too, and drinking himself to death was the best way he knew. Staying alive meant staying drunk.

'Yes,' he said slowly. 'Yes, Jack, I'm pissed. Completely pissed. I've decided to retire. Ill-health.'

Jack Singleterry hid his mouth behind his hand. He wasn't sure how to react. 'Not a wise move, Bill. You'll screw pension.'

Bill Naylor laughed: he'd not need a pension, and he'd evade the inevitable disciplinary tribunal. He'd hand in his notice, just like Mrs Eccles, and disappear. There was too much mess to clear up. 'I'm meant to be the one with problems, Jack, but you can't remember a bloody thing, can you?'

'What's the joke, pisshead?' demanded his immediate superior. Jack Singleterry would be lost without him.

'Us, Jack. It's not that funny. Remember Harry Noyes?'

'Stupid sod, digging brother's allotment for him – Big Charlie, pissed himself. Why should I remember? You were with me.'

'I were with you before,' Bill Naylor replied.

Last weekend he had remembered everything. Looking out of his kitchen window, he realized he had to sort out the garden before the neighbours' complaints to the council dragged him into court. Trying to zip up a pair of old trousers, he didn't just recall leaning on the Noyes boys, the interview that led them to Blank Frank Miller and the mess at Airport Van Hire. No, what came to him were memories from before his marriage, buying this house, over thirty years ago, when he and Singleterry were both just raw sergeants, dead keen to get results. They'd not noticed the scarring on Adtombwe's cheeks then, either.

From Singleterry's desk he picked the sharpest pencil he could find and held it in front of Singleterry. Facts on paper

185

meant results. He should know, he had written most of them down.

'No need to make notes, Bill.'

'Already have.'

'Get on with it then.'

'You rammed this straight up Harry Noyes' nostrils. Both of them.'

It seemed to take a while for Singleterry to remember why. He recalled beating him up after he had already confessed. Then he realized he didn't need to have a reason. 'Jesus Christ, Billy, that were thirty year ago. Is that all? Why the hell bring it up today? He were a scrote, we needed collar, you agreed. Are you wired?'

DCI Naylor had expected this. He offered to open out his jacket.

'That black-faced bitch Birtels not put you up to this? She hasn't the brains and you haven't the balls. Records say he had a nosebleed. Records say he fucking well confessed. Don't forget, you wrote them up.'

'I wasn't only thinking of Harold Noyes.'

In the interview room DC Wilet and DI Tilt waited for the locality mental health team. They did their best to explain to Nigal Adtombwe that this would help. Wreathed in a blanket, their prisoner shook his head. When he had refused to come out, or acknowledge their knocks and requests at the toilet door, they had opened its lock to find him huddled in a corner, shivering uncontrollably, clothes soaked in his own urine.

'They s-s-s-sent an ambulance to collect Jez. Three weeks after the funeral I went to the police to find out what had happened to him. I saw the two detectives who came to the school once they discovered the body. One was that man you work for . . . Sergeant Naylor.'

'Detective chief inspector,' corrected Tilt. He stopped. It

186

was too much of a coincidence. 'Just a moment. We're about to start the tapes again.' He read their prisoner his rights. Adtombwe nodded his head.

'No. He was a detective sergeant then.'

'What was his name?' asked Tilt. 'For the tape.'

'Detective Sergeant Naylor. There were two of them who came to the school after Jez was found dead in the washroom. I don't remember the other man's name. He was shouting outside the lavatory just now. Shouting at you, I heard his voice. It made me pee myself again – sorry, I didn't mean to.'

'That's all right,' Tilt replied quietly.

Adtombwe's body still shivered. Ruth Wilet walked over and draped another blanket gently over his shoulders.

'What happened next in the police station? Three weeks after the funeral.'

'I remember they left me in another interview room, to watch its clock tick for days. Then screams rushed down the corridor. Deep, dreadful screams. They howled and roared and sobbed. The shouting man swore and did something to make those big, dreadful screams roll all over again, worse, an animal caught in a trap. I wished I'd never come. I didn't know how to get back. There was blood on his hands. Blood on the pencil he took from his jacket.'

'Go on,' said DI Tilt, trying to quell the surprise in his voice. Surprise that Singleterry and Naylor were investigating officers in the death of Jeremy Rose. Not surprised that they may well have covered up their investigation. Buried it completely. No wonder Adtombwe had clammed up tight at his first interview after Tilt brought him in. He recognized Naylor – from thirty years ago. None of this need ever have happened, neither the murder nor the delay in getting to the bottom of it. For over thirty years Naylor and Singleterry had probably sat on vital evidence, but Tilt needed to be sure.

'What did you tell them?'

Nigal Adtombwe looked shocked. Surely Detective Inspector Funeral had checked their records. 'Everything. I told them everything. They wrote it down. Everything.'

Bill Naylor stared at the tip of the pencil. 'I was thinking of Jeremy Rose. You won't remember, Jack. You won't recall how he were found in washrooms of Green Three dormitory, the Cutlers' School, hanging by his dressing-gown cord. You didn't need to. I wrote it all down for you. I was your memory.'

'Just don't forget it then,' Singleterry ordered.

'Not to worry, Jack, I'll try not to. You know, we're getting to be as bad as each other, at writing things down. You wouldn't recollect our DI telling us to interview entire junior school, prep school they called it. Not real work, you said, not banging up scrotes.' He held the pencil in front of Jack Singleterry as though he was composing a still life. In a way he was. 'You don't have to remember, neither do I. Just go down to basement and have a look in the files for 1966. They're still more or less in order. You don't have to remember a twelve-year-old from Nigeria coming to the front desk a month later. You were too busy shoving a confession back up Harry Noyes' nose.' DCI Naylor dropped the pencil. 'Not that he actually did what he confessed to, mind.'

'Fuck you,' spat Singleterry. 'If I want lecture about police procedure, I'll go to that twat-faced cunt Tilt.'

'Good idea, he got the result. But this is between us. It's all in the files.' DCI Naylor unfolded three sheets of paper from inside his jacket pocket. 'Except this.'

While Adtombwe spoke, Tilt and Wilet exchanged looks. They were investigating their direct superiors.

'They told me they were detectives, and not to worry

about school. All I needed to do was state exactly what had happened. Provided it was the truth, they'd know what to do. They were policemen. I believed them. "You won't mention this to Mr Congreave," I said, after they started to write it down. "I don't want to get into trouble. I don't want him to get into trouble." They promised they wouldn't tell him. I couldn't stop myself once I began to tell them the truth.'

In the interview room the tape recorder picked up everything. Everything he had repeated to the two detective sergeants thirty-two years ago. Tilt checked it back with Adtombwe. It all made sense, dreadful sense. He used this space to phrase the next vital question.

'You made a signed statement?' the detective inspector asked with clinical care. He needed to know. Confirm the worst.

'Yes, I've already told you – Sergeant Naylor wrote it down, then read it back to me. The other sergeant watched. He and I signed at the bottom of the last page.'

The same people had buried the same case. Not once, but twice. Three decades apart, deep beneath Adtombwe's signature, deep beneath the deepest rivers of this city. It stank. Ruth Wilet and John Tilt did not think it could have been worse, except it was. Nigal Adtombwe was innocent then, and Peter Congreave guilty. Now it was the other way around.

How many other cases were left buried by these same people? For well over thirty years they had gone out of their way not to solve crime. They had reversed the law to turn justice inside out. To free the guilty and trap the innocent. These same people. How many cases had they twisted the truth out of? Detective Chief Inspector Naylor couldn't remember; Detective Superintendent Singleterry couldn't care less.

He stared at the three pages of copybook handwriting face up on his desk. He didn't bother to try and read a word of it. He was steadily becoming long-sighted and really required reading glasses, not that he ever read or wrote anything if he could help it. All his life he had denied dyslexia by bullying others. Glasses would scarcely have helped.

'Never one for paperwork, were you, Jack? Left it to me. Nigal Adtombwe made this statement thirty year back. I'll read it out for you if you like.' DCI Naylor flicked to the second page. 'Here we are. "Before he killed himself Jeremy told me he and Mr Congreave had sex lots of times during the term before."'

'Jumped up little darkie.'

'You said that then, Jack. Not in the records either. You said we'd get nowt but grief with an investigation.'

'Fuck-all witnesses, fuck-all evidence, fuck-all chance of proof. Darkie didn't even want us to mention it to anyone.'

'You're dead right, of course, Jack. No CPS to worry about then, no parents or legally responsible adults either. Our call. It was purely our decision.'

'We'd have to go to that snot-arsed school, grovel to that smarmy headmaster, who'd deny the sodding lot. Not to mention the other fucker, that wing-collared bow-tied shirt-lifter. Was he the senior one of those two crap heads? Crap heads, Bill.'

Naylor did not laugh. 'Somerville. Head of the senior school. Sir Harold Cedric St John Somerville. They gave him the knighthood after he retired.'

'Arseholes, the pair of them. Your Somerfuckerville would put in word, chief'd have our legs for breakfast.'

'Back into uniform, Jack. Trainspotters on M1 in plodmobile.' DCI Naylor steadied himself. 'You thought bury it. Billy Boy here'll rewrite page two to make sure it stays buried for keeps – dead easy to pull.'

'Don't try the innocent with me, Bill. We did it all the time. What is this? You're better than Tilt and his frigid little cunt, Wilet, and you bloody well know it. What's got into you, Naylor?'

'You, Jack. You. You and me.' Naylor shook his head. 'I should've stopped you then. We had open and shut case.'

'But you didn't. We agreed, Bill. We agreed.'

'Yes, it were wrong. This should be in the files. I said it were wrong.'

'You're too old and too pissed to preach.' Jack Single-terry avoided Naylor's stare. 'Not to me. They were all at it, arse bandits, the lot of them. Congreave and his Jeremy. Darkie said they enjoyed it.'

'Freddie Noyes enjoyed robbing banks with shooters. Didn't stop us trying to shoot him. You were too busy fitting people up to deal with real crime. You enjoyed sticking pencils up his brother's nose.'

'Don't give us this righteous shit. He'd have done the same to me.'

'Who wouldn't? We've clipped our women and beaten up men who beat theirs. You enjoy doing it.'

'It's the job. We both know that.'

'Then why didn't we wait one night outside the Cutlers' School and smack that Peter Congreave? We did it to other nonces.'

Singleterry turned to the window. 'It never works. Lock the sods up and chop off their bollocks.'

'We didn't manage either, Jack.' DCI Naylor proceeded carefully. He wanted Singleterry to react to him for once, so he could take control of the situation. 'You should thank Nigal Adtombwe for doing your castrating for you. We were so good we'd forgotten we ever buried the case in the first place. We fucked all witnesses, fucked all evidence – fucked any chance of proof. Cigarette?' A pause to allow Singleterry to catch up, to grow more incensed.

Naylor lit two cigarettes. He watched Singleterry tuck his shirt further into its waistband. He was just far enough away from his superior to avoid an initial fist. Virtually throughout their careers he had helped alter events after they occurred. Now he no longer knew why. The second cigarette burned by the edge of the desk. Its smoke drifted to the ceiling. Singleterry still didn't turn round.

'Congreave weren't just a nonce, he were good at what he did – like you, Jack. Just like you. Once local patrol find him sandblasted to death at Reddlewoods, we fuck up big time all over again. He's a serial sodomist and pederast, head of a child pornography ring as well as a public school. Never mind a serious dip into juvenile prostitution, here and abroad. Right good he were. DCS Birtels'll tell you.' The way they worked had created a monster. 'We might as well kick the nonces out of stir and throw away keys.' The cigarette burned into the desk varnish. 'It were a good case, Jack. We could've proved Adtombwe's statement. We'd've been backed. You knew that.'

Naylor let the cigarette burn. Jack Singleterry's preferred treatment of suspected child molesters was a lit cigarette to their genitals.

'You enjoy seeing people hurt about as much as hurting them yourself. Your little darkie went back hoping we'd keep our word. Some hope. You knew Congreave'd screw the living daylights out of him.'

'Don't talk bollocks. He's a fucking darkie and deserves everything he gets.'

'No, Jack. We unsolved the crime. By God, we let him do it. Just so you'd enjoy thinking about it – probably creamed yourself stupid.'

Jack Singleterry turned from the window. In one motion he went to thrust the cigarette into DCI Naylor's crotch. He wanted to screw Billy Boy and everyone else he had hated for eternity. The way they worked fed a monster which devoured all but fear and its own muck. It'd eat up everyone given time, as it had with Jack Singleterry.

A small black boy in short grey flannel trousers and the Cutlers' blazer walked back past the front desk of the city centre police station. In the Botanical Gardens he went up to people and asked them if they would listen. Take him away and listen, to him and the voices inside his head. He didn't want to go back. School and the police station frightened him. He couldn't go home. They took the boy back to the Cutlers'.

For weeks he lived in the fear and hope of seeing the two detective sergeants again. They didn't return. Weeks turned into months. He waited a year, but he already knew they'd never come back. He waited for his voice and balls to drop. Two years later they did. His headmaster ceased to ream his arsehole then.

Bill Naylor waited.

'Get up. Get up before I hit you again.'

Jack Singleterry did not move. Bill Naylor touched his own cheek with the back of his hand. The knuckles hurt.

'I said get up.'

Singleterry held out a hand; Naylor refused to take it. He stared at Singleterry and shook his head.

'*Get up!*' Naylor shouted again. They could wait all day. He had finished with helping Jack Singleterry.

'You've broken my fucking nose.'

'Good,' was all DCI Naylor needed to say. He stubbed his cigarette out on Singleterry's desk, a pause to regain his breath. 'Sorry, Jack. You deserved that. Thirty year back. I should've decked you then.'

Very slowly Singleterry rose from the floor. He didn't know what to do next. No one had managed to hit him before. It hurt.

'You're fucked, Naylor.'

'Sure. Complaint and disciplinary, they'll send those serious twats over from Leeds to boil all our balls in vinegar. I'll be on pension.'

'Give us the report, Bill.'

'You don't get it, do you?'

'Shut the fuck up and give me the report.'

'You still don't get it.'

'Now!'

Bill Naylor went to hand the last loose end across. Instead he tore it to shreds.

'It's a copy, Jack. Don't worry, I'm sure I've lost the original. Misfiled it in records. Can't remember where, though. Not for the life of me.'

'Fuck you. Why the fuck did you have to keep it?'

Naylor could barely stop laughing. 'That's funny, real funny. You told me to. Keep all originals, Bill, you said, just in case we need to – set someone up. We did and all. Don't look so thick, Jack. Thirty year ago. Congreave and Adtombwe, child abuser and murderer. Now that's right comic, that.'

'Stop laughing, Bill. You've just ruined your career.'

DCI Bill Naylor stopped laughing. 'Yes. Thirty year back. Ruin yours, mind.'

'You wrote report.'

'You signed it. Your signature next to his: "Jack Singleterry". Usually was, to take credit. Your name, your career, the toilet. You might get away with a suspended sentence, but I doubt it. Ex-coppers don't do too well in stir.'

'Christ, we've got out of worse than this.'

'Far worse, but thank you, no.'

'Why the fuck not? Why?'

'You enjoy making sure people stay hurt. I'm a policeman. You won't believe this, I don't really myself, but I came to work with same idea as John Tilt once. Your nose is dripping blood onto your desk, by the way. To uphold the law for the good of people. You left him with this case because you thought he'd never crack it. Our job was to protect the world from the likes of you and Congreave.'

'Evil fucking bastard.'

'Who? Him? You? Me? We probably are. We good as murdered the pair of them.' Tears welled in Bill Naylor's eyes. 'We did it in the end though, Jack. Got result. Or Tilt did. Oh yes, nearly forgot. Someone else asked for a copy.'

'Who?'

'Nigal Adtombwe, when he were twelve years old. "No, son," you said. "It's safer with us."'

Nigal Adtombwe pulled himself back into the blankets until only his face showed. Tears rained down his cheeks. They were rivers that had sculpted the past without washing it away.

'They broke their word. Mr Congreave led me into his study. It was late. I told him I'd been out for a walk to think about Jez – and I'd forgotten to look at my watch. He knew he ought to set me an imposition but he said he understood all about Jeremy. He locked the door with a smile. I smelled the hunger beneath the aftershave. His hands turned up the sound of the television, then loosened my trousers and bent me over. A ciné camera started to whirr. Before his cock went up my arse I thought he was going to cane me.'

DC Wilet wanted to hold across tissue after tissue to wipe away the tears. Nigal's did not stop; she held back her own. Thirty-odd years of hiding had buried nothing. The truth didn't do anyone any good; no one could stop Singleterry and Naylor. They had let Congreave get away with it, let him trap Nigal Adtombwe for ever. It was too late to help or punish. There was no justice, and now she realized there never had been.

DI Tilt drew a deep breath to try and draw the interview to a close. 'So you killed him. Will you confirm that on the night of Saturday 24 January 1998, you did murder Peter Congreave? For the tape.'

Their prisoner dried his face in the blanket to stare at each of them in turn. The recording needles of the tape recorder waited for an answer. A strange calm, close to dying, passed through the air.

'Yes,' Nigal Adtombwe finally replied. 'I'm guilty. I killed him, killed him, killed him. He is dead. I've killed him, haven't I?' For an instant he seemed composed. 'I am guilty. They took away my innocence.'

He stopped. His eyes glazed over again. They shrank into a blankness they did not comprehend.

DI Tilt checked his watch and read out the time. Their prisoner seemed to be relapsing into a catatonic state. There was no time to take it all in now. He had to check where the locality mental health team were. They'd need its qualified social worker to complete a section, for the patient's sake. He nodded to Ruth Wilet to stop the tapes.

Suddenly Nigal Adtombwe spoke.

'I've not told you *how* I killed him. I want to now.' Pain flashed across his face. 'He said he didn't think I'd want to hurt him. It was all a big mistake and he had to leave. He had a train to catch. He can't have heard me. Not listened. Not accepted one word. That hurt.'

Rain hammered against the corrugated roof. Cold, hard, almost ice. Peter Congreave had taken enough. He wanted to smash Adtombwe into a bloody pulp.

'Untie me.'

'No.' His captor did not know why he said it. 'I am going to kill you.'

Congreave laughed. 'With what?'

Adtombwe pointed to the sandblaster.

'No, no,' he replied. 'With what inside your head? Don't you understand, Nigal? You're a victim. Victims are too weak to kill. That's why they are victims. Believe me, I know you better than yourself.'

Which was true – up till then.

Congreave tried to dodge the flash of the Polaroid. 'What are you doing?' Too late.

'I want to show you who you are.' The Polaroid curled out of the camera like a tongue. Adtombwe counted off the seconds then stripped away the layer of spent chemicals. Slowly Congreave's image spilled out in front of them. He's in my film now, thought his victim. Congreave didn't stop to look at himself.

John Tilt remembered the first Polaroid. The victim's face. Perfect, except for the blood around an eye. A look without emotion. Without feeling. Why not? Why not kill Peter Congreave? He raped children then ravaged their lives for ever. Children we gave him to care for. He grew and fed on the pain of their suffering which his vile body inflicted, then hid.

Without a faith, John Tilt answered his own question. Kill him. Evil deserves to die. Sandblast him to death, Nigal Adtombwe. Go on, kill him. You have nothing left to lose, except the pain. There is no redemption.

It was no coincidence they had met at Congreave's funeral. No accident he had confessed to the detective inspector then. '*Unto me is this grace given, that I should preach among the Gentiles the unsearchable riches of Christ; and to make all men see what is the fellowship of the mystery, which from the beginning of the world hath been hid in God, who created all things.*' They had both believed in a God. They had both believed in a world better than the one they knew. The rest is madness.

197

Nigal Adtombwe had stopped. But there was more to come, Tilt knew. Something their prisoner had wanted to tell them, before he went to the toilet. About the boy hanging from that other toilet door. Tell us, Tilt was about to say, desperate to reach the end, but Adtombwe had already decided to tell them everything he had discovered on the night of Saturday 24 January.

Trying to find a way out, Peter Congreave eyed up the sandblaster. 'What is this?' he asked in the voice of a scared child.

Nigal Adtombwe did not have to lie or pretend. 'A hydro-pneumatic steel finishing tool. It's set to inflict little immediate damage. It'll take time. You'll feel the pain you forced into others.'

Tied to himself, Peter Congreave tried to outstare the tip of the tool. Piss drooled from his cock onto the floor. It puddled around his feet.

Adtombwe no longer cared. 'Don't worry,' he said. 'It will hurt.'

'You're mad.'

In the interview room and behind the sandblaster Nigal nodded his head. 'Yes. You're evil.'

'Stop!'

'No.'

Congreave screamed. Adtombwe wanted him to stop. He hadn't started yet.

'Nigal, don't punish me, I can't help it. Paedophile, pederast; names hardly hurt. Did I try to hurt you? Was I cruel? Did I do anything to anyone against their will? They want me for who I am. Jeremy did. You, in your strange way, even today. If I say I'll never touch another boy, will you untie me? I can't. I've a wife, children, grandchildren. It's torture to touch them as I touch others. I remain a good teacher, a good husband and father, if not a good man. I don't preach, I shan't plead. I've never judged others as they might judge me. Is it my fault God made me this way? Do you think I asked to be like this?'

'Did He ask you to bugger us?' Adtombwe wanted to leave him alone, but couldn't. 'You'd never listen. Did Jez ever ask you to stop, Mr Congreave? No, he couldn't, you couldn't let him. He managed to speak to you, though.' Inside his head Nigal Adtombwe kept hearing footsteps down the corridor to the washroom. 'He told you that night, didn't he? You helped him when he said he wanted to kill himself.'

Congreave closed his eyes and took his time. He answered very clearly. He had just realized he had to die. Adtombwe waited behind the sandblaster to hear the truth.

'To save pain. Jeremy was hurting so much. To save us all pain. He'd talk, say the wrong things. He asked me to. He wanted to kill himself. Perhaps I helped him on his way. To tie the cord of his dressing gown and kick away the bucket. Out of compassion. Believe me, out of compassion.'

Detective Constable Wilet watched her detective inspector remain motionless. She remembered the rusting coldness of the gantry rail edge into her fingers. She saw John Tilt lift the regulation incident sheet, then nothing. Nothing but the mutilated face and body of Peter Congreave. Ruth did not want anybody to die except when they needed to. Adtombwe had created their memories, sculpted them from his own. It was a work of art.

Nigal Adtombwe's fingernails tried to dig out his own skull. 'It hurts. Inside it hurts. I want to open up my brain and rip it out. It hurts.' He fought against himself to pull his arms down till his fists pressed against the table.

'I don't want to remember what he said. I never meant to hurt him; the noise inside my head forced me to. Just frighten him a little, help him understand what we've been through. Gain some peace from these voices. I want them to end. I want the misery to end. I switched on the motors to start to take him out of his, then something dark passed over us. I clipped on a filter, flicked down the visor, to see him as this creature we'd become. And I couldn't stop.

'I had to remove the feel of his skin from the parts of the body which first touched ours. Hands, which he tried to hide between his legs, and his screams. I'd pushed Jez aside: he's dead now. In all the noise I tried to blast away the smell of his aftershave. Each time the screaming stopped I removed the mask and visor and the camera lens-cap to take a picture. I don't know why. I showed them to him, like those ciné films of his. He needed to know what we'd turned into. To see the creature for himself. He begged me to stop. I didn't. I couldn't. I had become him.'

The sandblaster moved over each part of his body that had touched others – lips, chest, thighs, to where Adtombwe's fist had nearly smashed into his face. It turned him more and more into the creatures that screamed inside Adtombwe's head. The weight of material slowly spun the turntable around and around. He tried to hide. The sandblaster moved to the next part of his body, the crotch. Hands attempt to chase pain, but they move too slowly between screams to block the agony. The smell of sweat and burnt flesh eats into the smell of creased paper. Gradually his genitals and face disappear. The sandblaster rips off his mask. With each layer of skin the more real the creature becomes.

His throat starts to cry out for the camera. Each Polaroid a break in the torment. His words begin to break up, split into the shreds of skin his assailant cleans from the camera lens. It seems to take hours. The sandblaster leaves his eyes till last. Blind, he still cries out for the camera until he yells and coughs no more. Flesh and blood ooze from the remains of his eyes and mouth. He breathes like an animal through a face of blood, a beast. There is nothing else left. Just the creature they have created. The noise stops when the film runs out.

The blasting bay becomes darker. Snow outside fills the panels in the roof, to blanket the moon. Adtombwe switches off the lights and power. In the torch beam he still expects the person sitting on the chair to be alive and dressed.

Instead there is just a creature.

Twenty

They thought they recognized each other walking down the paths to the wooden footbridge at the end of the valley. The city lay out of sight, quarantined by protective hills. Summer was just starting to shift into autumn. The foot and mouth restrictions which had closed the countryside to the outside world for months had only just been lifted. At least the footpaths were open.

It took them a while for their paths to cross and come together. It had already taken several years. Reddlewood Steel Finishers was an empty name, while Carrdyke Lane lay buried under brown-site redevelopment: an organic wholefood distributor, next to a creative industries quarter for ethnic minorities, including recording and artists' studios. The case was history. Blasting bay six no longer existed.

Ruth Wilet tried hard not to stare at her former boss. He was looking far older and smaller than she remembered. She had never seen him off duty before. John Tilt held his younger daughter's hand. DC Wilet was dressed in the olive green of a park ranger. She seemed to have swopped one uniform for another, except they had never worn uniforms when they had worked together.

DI Tilt had not left the police force immediately: he felt obliged to stay on and at least see the trial through to its end. After the trial City Section was disbanded pending an internal inquiry, and his transfer to records became permanent.

The inquiry exonerated City Section. Bill Naylor was promoted to superintendent and took early retirement on medical grounds. Three months later he became the civilian Director of Studies at the new Home Office-funded Northern Police Training Academy.

Detective Superintendent Jack Singleterry stayed in the force. He was asked to join the Yorkshire Region Police Corruption Unit, and agreed only on condition that he outranked its other senior officer, Detective Chief Superintendent Celene Birtels. Deputy Commander Singleterry's word was law. He and Bill Naylor never spoke to each other again.

Tilt remained in records, supervising the burial of countless investigations, good or bad. He was told to keep his mouth shut, otherwise as investigating officer in the Reddlewood case he would have to face a disciplinary and take the blame for any misdemeanours and errors in procedure, criminal charges notwithstanding. He stared at the chief constable and started the slow countdown to his fiftieth birthday and early retirement without loss of pension rights.

It was more than just a whitewash or a cover up. While DI Tilt sat in records, the city police force formulated a policy and strategy to promote corruption, and it worked. Too many personal careers and institutional reputations lay at risk to do otherwise.

DC Wilet was transferred to the Derbyshire Constabulary, where she worked as a schools liaison officer. She had left plainclothes, guns, violence and fit-ups for ever. She acted as a seasonal ranger by volunteering outside the shift pattern and during holidays. She hated the force. She and Rachael Sissens split up a year after Adtombwe was arrested. Their relationship had started to break down the day Rachael's car witnessed the maiming of Colin Clemp at Airport Van Hire. In the end Rachael left in a hurry because Ruth had hit her during an argument, hard enough to need seven stitches over the eye. 'I can change,' Ruth had pleaded. 'You know I can change.'

'Yes,' replied her ex-lover, 'that's what frightens me. I'm not coming back.'

Wilet had kept her notes from DI Tilt's lectures when she had first joined the police force: 'From Crime to Conviction'. It seemed prehistory to her when she was outside, surrounded by rocks, streams and fields. She had twenty more years before early retirement and she still dreamt she was stumbling down a diagonal of tiles that led to a deserted factory building off Carrdyke Lane. It was a life sentence.

Tilt retired, with thoughts of saving his marriage and faith. He had managed neither. The church had asked him to consider training for the priesthood but he did not know where to begin. He had no faith. Just the idea of worship scared him, though he was too frightened to admit it, even to himself. The same was true of his marriage: there was nothing left to save. His wife was arranging a divorce by mutual separation: nisi would become absolute in six months' time. They shared their children as best they could.

He had nearly managed to bury the investigation itself. Throughout the trial Mrs Congreave had sat in the visitors' gallery as impassively stone-faced as Nigal Adtombwe himself. DI Tilt had interviewed her over and over again to ascertain whether she was aware of her husband's behaviour outside the marital bed. Charges might be preferred but not without firm evidence. For some reason he needed to know. Her solicitor called when they failed to appear for interview. She was in intensive care, a massive overdose of aspirin, still on the critical list. There were bruises around her face where she had beaten herself with a small crematorial urn. John Tilt visited her in hospital and knew.

He and Ruth Wilet stood at each end of the footbridge. The sun had turned the sky a bleached shade of red, the stream rippling underneath the reused railway sleepers a polished russet brown. They made eye-contact and decided to say nothing. It was too late to speak.

The approach of twilight had caused the dew of a thousand tiny cobwebs to shimmer from grass blade to grass blade far across the meadowland. Because of foot and mouth it was ungrazed, which only heightened the effect. Each glistening strand shivered slightly with the touch of motion that colder air fetches from the shaded side of a valley.

'It's beautiful,' Tilt's daughter told her father, who nodded his head. The patterns reminded him of the whorls of spent abrasive surrounding Congreave's body. He needed to hold his daughter's hand while they watched the evening tuck its covers over their city. Ruth Wilet walked past without a word.

Safe inside Daddy's car, Laura Tilt followed its headlights as they chased streams from valley to valley into deeper valleys and down into the city, while the night moved on inside the dark. Her father listened to her fall asleep in the back seat. Nigal Adtombwe was Laura's age when he had first come to Sheffield.

Her father kept asking himself if he'd still be free had they not met at the funeral. The last time he travelled down to the special hospital he had gone with Nigal Adtombwe's other visitor. The patient never smiled, rarely spoke. The shuffling walk, slurred gait and speech, the slow motion movement were not entirely due to his medication. He had regressed.

Even before the trial he had continued to deteriorate. The

periods of lucidity shrank into moments. The voices inside his head took over the outbursts of hurried mumblings between immense spells of rigid catatonic stares. To kill Congreave made sense. Doing it drove Adtombwe mad. It let the dead control his mind. Without warning or reason, he started to assault others: extreme, uncontrolled violence to anyone who tried to come too close. 'Go away,' he yelled at them. 'I want to kill everyone. Go away.' Perhaps he was trying to protect them from Congreave. But, as he himself had said, he had become Congreave.

The medication appeared to hold back the violence. By the time he was sent to Broadmoor his personality had disappeared. John Tilt had watched it gradually vanish, worn away, like the stone face of a statue eaten up in the atmosphere of a caustic city. Tilt had lost his faith, Adtombwe his entire being. He no longer recognized Detective Inspector Funeral. He only spoke in the voices of creatures. He attacked himself. He was clearly insane.

Staff at Broadmoor found it difficult to believe he had been a sculptor. They no longer attempted to interest him in their workshops and studios. The other patients steered well clear. They knew they were all in the forensic hospital because they were a danger to themselves and others. But he was too scary, too bleak an unknown. A consultant psychiatrist did raise the possibility of a transfer by Home Office Licence. The place did not seem to suit him. His presence seemed to disturb the other patients and staff; it was dreadful to watch someone sandblast everything left inside their skull. He still listened to everything. They pulled him off the consultant; a massive injection of tranquillizers in the backside restrained the outburst. He seemed steadfast in his denial that he could be a person. Whoever he was before, he could not be reached while he tried to obliterate himself. He never recognized staff, patients or visitors.

He had become nothing.

Through a washroom window he sees a moon shine through falling snow. He does not see his visitors leave.

Tilt shared a taxi to the railway station with the other visitor. 'It's like the Cutlers',' Mrs Congreave said after they'd been checked through the security gates. They had met again directly after the trial. To end the investigation it had been necessary to return those of her husband's belongings the police had been able to recover, plastic-bagged close to a year to the day after her husband had last taken them off. She held them to her chest, and he let her hold him as she finally let herself cry and cry and cry. They said nothing. Neither he nor she knew what else to do.

Their paths crossed once more after he had left the police force, at a preview of a retrospective exhibition of Nigal Adtombwe's work at the new Millennium Gallery. It had been arranged by Imogen Tuille, who mourned the artist rather than the man. They had been invited together. 'It was the least we could do,' she told them. 'He has nothing else left.' They had arranged to travel down to the West Country and visit together. At the railway station they promised to keep in touch.